The Deal Breaker

The Billionaires of Silicon Forest, Book Three

MELISSA McCLONE

The Deal Breaker
The Billionaires of Silicon Forest (Book 3)
Copyright © 2020 Melissa McClone

ALL RIGHTS RESERVED

The unauthorized reproduction or distribution of this copyrighted work, in any form by any electronic, mechanical, or other means, is illegal and forbidden, without written permission of the author, except in the case of brief quotations embodied in critical articles and reviews.

This is a work of fiction. Characters, settings, names, and occurrences are products of the author's imagination or used fictitiously and bear no resemblance to any actual person, living or dead, places or settings and/or occurrences. Any incidences of resemblance are purely coincidental.

Cover by Elizabeth Mackay

Cardinal
PRESS

Cardinal Press, LLC
January 2020

Dedication

For my daughter Mackenna
Thanks for helping me brainstorm this series and
especially Iris and Dash's story.

Chapter One

As the clock struck midnight, poker night at Dash Cabot's house ended. Relief surged through him, but his tense shoulders didn't loosen. The scent of alcohol, the remnants inside glasses, hung in the air. Nothing beat an evening with his seven closest friends—and tonight was no exception—but he was ready to say goodbye to his family by choice and send them home.

Someone said good night—Brett Matthews, who owned an investment firm in downtown Portland. So far, he was the only one with a baby, but Dash had a feeling more of their group would be on the track to parenthood soon.

Kieran O'Neal and Mason Reese followed Brett to the front door.

Three down, four to go.

Dash wouldn't kick out the remaining ones. He'd needed this impromptu poker night as much as the others, who worked hard at their companies and firms. Well, except for Henry Davenport, who'd inherited his money.

Blaise Mortenson said something and then laughed before elbowing Wes Lockhart.

Wes groaned. "Uncle jokes are worse than dad ones."

"Just wait until you marry Paige and become an official uncle." Blaise elbowed him. "You'll beg for my punchlines."

"That will never happen." Wes grabbed his jacket. "I can come up with jokes on my own."

Across the room, Adam Zeile laughed before waving goodbye. "Cambria is waiting up for me. I need to get home."

About time.

Dash wasn't sure if he'd thought the words or said them aloud. No one glanced his way with a frown, so that was good. Sometimes he said the wrong things or people took his words the wrong way. Around the guys, Dash could be himself, but after a long week of attending meetings and dinners, dealing with issues on a new project, and being forced to act "professional," he'd had enough socializing.

His shirt collar irritated him. He'd rolled up his sleeves before letting them down more times than he could count, and his muscles twitched. He wanted to put on sweats, a hoodie, and escape into a video game.

Instead, he put away the cards and chips. Sure, he could have left them for the morning, but he needed to do something or he'd be tempted to say "get out."

Not unusual for him.

He wasn't rude on purpose, but his brain functioned ten steps ahead of everyone else and, even then, what he wanted to say didn't always come out the way he intended. He was trying to do better. In some cases, he'd succeeded, like when someone needed him. Dash had risen to the occasion when Wes was an idiot with his now-fiancée, Paige, and after Blaise told them about his parents being drug addicts.

The front door closed.

One more gone.

Henry Davenport topped off his glass.

Dash sighed. He would have expected Henry—who'd never worked a day in his life yet had the highest net worth in the group—to have left already. The guy usually had a date lined up after their poker night ended.

Be patient.

Dash pressed his lips together. No reason to eye his gaming system yet. Only three remained. Their discussion over the latest change to the country's interest rate wouldn't last long.

In a few minutes, he would be alone. Then, he could stay up all night and play video games to make up for the time he'd lost to…adulting.

Most people had no idea what being a billionaire meant. Sure, some like Henry did nothing but spend or give away their money. He could do that because others like Brett and Blaise grew his investments. The others, including Dash, ran or were on the board of the companies they founded. He could work twenty-four hours a day and still have more to do. Which was why his Friday night gaming time was sacred even when he had a date with his girlfriend, Raina, or his friends got together.

Blaise pocketed his winnings. He hadn't counted the money, but Dash bet the guy knew the exact amount.

"I can't wait to do this again." Blaise's smirk grew. "It's like getting candy on Halloween, but no trick-or-treating required."

"Luck," Henry countered. "And you didn't win that much."

"Skill." Blaise flashed a lopsided grin. "And yes, I did."

Dash never took a side, but Blaise usually won because of his fine-tuned poker skills. The money, however, went to a school program that sent food home each weekend with kids who qualified for free lunch. Dash knew this because his assistant, Blaise's sister-in-law, Fallon, had mentioned it at work. But it

THE DEAL BREAKER

made sense since Blaise had once been a kid who went hungry more often than not.

Blaise shrugged on his coat. "Thanks for hosting, Wonderkid."

Dash fought a grimace. He hated the nickname. That wasn't the only one his friends had for him, either. Mr. Status Quo was another. But being teased was the drawback of being the youngest and smartest of the eight. Despite that, he wouldn't trade the guys for anything.

"No problem." *I should lighten up.* Finding time to get together wasn't as easy now that five were married and one was engaged. "We need to do this more often."

"We do." Blaise removed his gloves from his pocket. Rain fell most days, typical for January, but a cold front had brought freezing temperatures and predictions of snow. "Talk to you on the group chat. Ready, Wes?"

Wes nodded and then waved goodbye. The two headed toward the front door. That left...

Henry placed his glass on the counter and headed toward the back door.

Muscles bunching, Dash blocked Henry's path. "You're going the wrong way."

"I'm not leaving." A smug smile spread across Henry's face. "Iris is expecting me."

At midnight? No way.

Dash balled his hands. He wasn't one for

violence. Ever since his parents' bitter divorce, he'd done what he could to avoid confrontation, honing his skills as a referee and a peacemaker to handle his parents. Sometimes those worked well with his friends. But he was ready to punch Henry in the face or the gut or anywhere else required. The billionaire trust fund baby—if a man in his early thirties could be called a baby—had no reason to be alone with Iris in the guest cottage at this hour.

Or any other time.

Henry Davenport wasn't good enough for Iris Jacobs.

Sweet, caring, hardworking Iris.

Dash had met her when they were thirteen, and they became best friends. They were now twenty-eight. Not much had changed since they were teenagers except she'd worked for him as his housekeeper and cook for the past six years.

Iris was the one person he could count on no matter what. Dash couldn't say that about his parents. He wouldn't allow Henry to mess with her. Break her heart. Steal her away.

His friends joked about hiring Iris, but Dash knew she'd never leave him. They'd been through so much together and relied on each other.

Friends forever.

That had been their deal.

But seeing her kiss Henry on New Year's Eve, two weeks ago, had shocked Dash in a way he still didn't understand.

Iris, however, hadn't said a word about the kiss, so he assumed whatever had happened between her and Henry was nothing more than getting caught up in celebrating. Dash had been so relieved, like the-sun-appearing-after-months-of-rain relieved. But now...

He squared his shoulders. "Iris is asleep."

"You don't know that."

Dash didn't because he couldn't see the cottage from here, but he would do what he could to protect her. "Earlier, she mentioned being tired."

"Iris gives a hundred and ten percent." Henry's gaze softened. "She did a wonderful job with the food and drinks, as usual."

"She's never let me down."

Iris was the most important person in his life. He had to keep her heart safe from Henry, who could be the poster boy for Peter Pan Syndrome. The guy never took life seriously. He might be a well-known and respected philanthropist and one of Dash's closest friends, but Henry didn't believe in commitment. He preferred having fun to being serious.

"Me, either." Henry grinned.

The smug tone sent Dash's blood pressure spiraling. Henry could be immature. Maybe simple and direct was the best strategy. "Leave Iris alone. If you break her heart, I'll be the one picking up the pieces. I'm all she has."

As Henry tilted his chin, disbelief shone in his gaze. "You're all she has?"

Dash straightened. "Yes."

"Then why did you forget about her over the holidays? Leave her in this big house without a present to open on Christmas morning?"

Each word deflated him because what Henry said was true. Dash had been so busy working and then visiting Raina's family on the East Coast, he hadn't considered how Iris would spend the holidays with him away. He'd forgotten her and their Christmas Day tradition. He hadn't even bought her a gift. When he'd arrived home, he'd found a present from her under the tree.

"It slipped my mind," Dash admitted.

Henry rolled his eyes. "It? You mean Iris."

"I apologized." The words shot out. Dash had promised to make it up to her on her birthday. He'd also written her a six-figure bonus check. Normally, Iris would have laughed and ripped it up. Not this time. She'd said thank you and deposited the check the next day. "She forgave me."

"Of course she did, because that's what Iris does. It's her nature. Something that has nothing to do with you." Henry didn't sound impressed. "You might reconsider telling people you're all she has when it was everyone else who made sure Iris wasn't alone for Christmas when you dropped the ball."

Dash's face burned. "It won't happen again."

"No, it won't."

Henry's strong words hit like a sucker punch. Dash forced himself to breathe. "What do you mean?"

Henry shrugged.

Dash stepped forward, using his height advantage. He might be the youngest, but he was also the tallest. "What are your intentions with Iris, dude?"

Henry laughed. "Intentions and dude do not belong in the same sentence."

"I'm not kidding." This was out of Dash's comfort zone, but he couldn't back down. "You're going to hurt Iris. There are other women you can date. Leave her alone."

"Oh, Dashiell." Henry tsked after saying Dash's full name. "You're jealous and allowing the green-eyed monster to get the best of you."

Dash's jaw dropped. "I'm not. I have a girlfriend."

Henry sighed. "You're still dating Raina?"

Dash nodded.

"Pity."

What? He couldn't let Henry diss his girlfriend. "Raina is nice. She's pretty, smart, and a world-class gamer."

"Yes, but she isn't the one for you."

Dash stiffened. "She's perfect for me. Hadley—"

"Hadley is an excellent matchmaker, but not all

the couples she introduces get married."

"I didn't mention marriage." Dash should have realized Henry was trying to get a rise out of him. The guy was never serious. "I'm only dating Raina."

"And missing out on what's right underneath your nose," Henry muttered.

"Huh?"

"Never mind. Since you are 'dating'"—Henry made quote marks with his fingers around the last word—"why do you care so much about what Iris does?"

With me.

Henry hadn't spoken the words, but he might as well have.

Heat rushed up Dash's neck. "She has no family. Her mom's dead. Her father deserted her to marry a woman half his age. We look out for each other."

"She runs your household and your life."

"Yes, and she does an excellent job at both. I pay her well." Iris also lived rent-free in the two-bedroom guest house in his backyard—one of her benefits. "But she's...fragile."

Henry laughed. "Iris is one of the strongest women I've ever met."

"She doesn't go out much." Dash wasn't sure why not, but he hadn't wanted to pry into her dating habits. They'd never discussed that part of her life. "The way you go through women—"

"I'm only trying to help her."

"By kissing her?"

"Still hung up on that New Year's Eve kiss?" Henry sounded amused.

Kisses, but who had been counting? Still, Dash didn't—couldn't—say anything.

"I don't blame you." Henry appeared more smug than usual. "Iris kisses better than she cooks."

Dash swallowed around the grapefruit-sized lump in his throat. He'd never kissed Iris. Once, they'd come close in high school. Thankfully, he'd come to his senses before ruining their friendship.

Just friends.
Forever friends.

He hadn't thought about kissing her since then. But seeing her with…

Henry laughed. "Your eyes are turning green, Wonderkid."

Dash crossed his arms over his chest. "Are you seeing other women besides Iris?"

"Are you proposing to Raina?"

The non sequitur made him do a double take. "What?"

"Are you planning to ask your girlfriend to marry you?" Henry clarified.

Dash let the question sink in. That left him with one of his own. "Why would I do that?"

"You've been dating Raina for months." Henry didn't mask his disapproval. He stepped closer until he was almost in Dash's face. "You spent Christmas with her family back east. She keeps dropping hints."

Dash rolled his eyes. The guy had it all wrong if he thought the last of the Silicon Forest Billionaires would get down on bended knee with a million-dollar engagement ring in hand. He took a step back. "Now that it's down to me and Wes, she's been obsessed about the bet. We haven't discussed marriage."

And wouldn't if Dash had his way.

Not appearing convinced, Henry rubbed his neck. "I should have joined the bet. There's no way I would have lost."

I won't, either.

More than five years ago, the six of them known as the Billionaires of Silicon Forest made a bet—the last single man standing won. Adam, Blaise, Kieran, Mason, Wes, and Dash each put ten million dollars into a fund that Blaise used to beta test a new investment algorithm. Since then, the money had grown to over six hundred million. Only two remained single—Dash and Wes, who got engaged on Christmas Day, but a wedding date hadn't been set.

"We asked you," Dash reminded. "Your answer was an emphatic no."

"I must have had a reason, but that's not what we're discussing. The bet is about you tech guys getting married, so are you proposing?"

"No," Dash admitted. "Marriage isn't part of my near-term plans."

"Define near-term."

Not ever.

His parents' divorce had not only thrown his stable world into upheaval, but fifteen years later, his mom and dad still used Dash as a pawn. They'd been so in love, but that had disintegrated into a battle no one could win. To this day, he continued to be a casualty of their war, and he never wanted to be like them.

That meant staying single.

Not that being unmarried was a hardship. He had Iris, who was better than a wife. She cooked, cleaned, shopped, did his laundry, laid out his clothes each night, and whatever else he might need without him having to make compromises or mess up his schedule. No woman, including Raina, could ever take care of him and his house as well as Iris did.

Which was why entering the bet had been a no-brainer when Mason proposed the wager. Dash had been twenty-three and the newest billionaire of the bunch.

Henry stared, waiting for an answer.

Dash shifted his weight between his feet. "Not this year or next."

Lines creased Henry's forehead. The guy appeared almost concerned, which was weird. Superficial seemed more his style. "Does Raina know that?"

"I mentioned it to her when we first went out." Dash hated feeling as if he were on the defensive.

He'd spent too many years in that position. Even now, his parents cross-examined him about each other whenever they spoke. "She was okay with it."

"Of course she was fine with it then." Henry spoke fast. "You need to remind her in case she's changed her mind or fallen in love with you."

Love? Dash gulped. "She's never said—"

"Doesn't mean she can't feel that way." Henry shook his head. "For being so smart, Dashiell, sometimes you can't see what's right in front of your face."

"I see Raina."

Henry stared at Dash with an odd expression before blowing out a breath.

Nothing new. People often treated him like an anomaly. Or a weirdo. He was used to it.

"Are we finished?" Henry asked. "Iris is waiting for me."

"Fine." Dash moved aside but then followed Henry outside, not bothering with a jacket. His breath hung on the air. Goose bumps covered his skin.

Henry glared over his shoulder. "She's waiting for me."

We'll see about that. "I never told her good night."

And if Dash's presence kept Henry from kissing Iris again, all the better.

Chapter Two

Where was Henry?

Iris peered out the cottage's front window. Lights illuminated the path leading to the door, but the swaying of a tree branch was the only movement in the backyard. She hoped he would have been here by now.

Was poker night still going?

She couldn't check because none of the windows or doors faced the main house. That gave her privacy, which she appreciated most of the time, but she wanted to know if people were there or if Dash had kicked them out so he could play video games.

If that was the case, maybe Henry changed his mind about stopping by. No, he might be self-absorbed, but he wasn't rude. More likely, he was taking his sweet time.

As usual.

Henry had a habit of being late. He claimed it was on purpose—to make an entrance—but Iris wasn't convinced. He wore an expensive watch, but he barely glanced at it. Instead, he seemed to lose track of time. She'd noticed that over the holidays.

Christmas.

Her chest tightened.

She shouldn't complain. No matter how tired she was, Henry could be as late as he wanted. He'd earned that right.

He and his friends had kept her from having a horrible time while Dash was away. Blaise and Hadley Mortenson had invited Iris to spend Christmas Eve and Day with them, but Henry had gone overboard the rest of the time, being a cross between an elf from Santa's Workshop and the living embodiment of Christmas spirit.

Iris had known little about him other than his larger-than-life persona usually left a smile on her face at parties she'd worked for Dash and his friends. But then Henry had swooped in like a white knight on a loyal steed—albeit a limousine—to save her from having a blue Christmas.

Though her situation—a dead mom and a father who deserted her—was different from Henry's, he understood about not having any family. His parents were dead. And like her, he was an only child.

Maybe that explained why they hit it off and became friends so quickly. People called him a partier and a player, but he'd shown her only kindness and compassion. Yes, the guy acted over-the-top, but that was likely a defense mechanism to mask his loneliness. She'd been lonely, too.

Which was why when Henry told her he wanted to make someone jealous at Dash's New Year's Eve party, she'd agreed to kiss him. More than once, even.

There'd been no spark or heat. Not surprising, since they were nothing more than friends. But the kiss had been pleasant.

Maybe he wanted to tell her his plan worked. She hoped that was the case. Henry gave so much of himself to people and to charities. He deserved to live happily ever after.

Iris yawned. She just wished he would get here. Staying up was becoming more difficult by the minute. She wanted to change into her fleece pajamas, crawl into bed, and sleep.

According to the clock on the bookshelf, it was eight after twelve.

Still early for eight billionaires playing poker on a Friday, but late for a housekeeper who needed to be up in the morning to clean up their mess. She'd occasionally worked for many of them at parties, but none were as needy as Dash, who relied on her to do everything for him.

Always had, even before he became so successful.

But not for much longer...

She plopped onto the overstuffed love seat. That was why she was so tired tonight.

Normally, she had an endless supply of energy, but the weight of her decisions these past weeks pressed against her shoulders like hundred-pound bags of flour. Preparing the food and drinks for the poker game had exhausted her. More than once, she'd leaned against the counter to rest for a few minutes.

Dash hadn't noticed.

Once upon a time, he would have and asked her what was wrong. They'd been best friends, and they'd made a deal that was never supposed to change, but it had. Slowly over the years, she went from being both his friend and employee to his domestic help. Iris did her job so well, she'd become invisible to him.

The familiar pain in her heart intensified.

He was all she had, but only two things mattered to Dash now—his company and Raina.

It was time for Iris to break their deal.

Put herself first.

Move on.

Start over.

She swallowed a sigh. Making new friends wouldn't be easy, but she would do what it took to create a new life on her own. Dash had created a family with his friends. That was what she wanted, too. If only she hadn't waited...

But her friendship with Dash had been enough,

so had taking care of him.

Until it wasn't.

His preferring to hang out with billionaires and intellectuals shouldn't surprise her. She wasn't like them or Raina, who was smart and beautiful and funny and designed the video games Dash loved so much. Still, Iris had believed that didn't matter to him.

But it had and did.

Dash spending Christmas with his girlfriend had been the wake-up call Iris needed. Okay, it had been more like a punch to the gut. He'd known she would be alone for the holidays, but he hadn't called or texted. Not even on Christmas Day. And when she'd placed her gift to him under his tree, she'd realized he'd truly forgotten her.

Fifteen years of friendship.

Of growing up together.

Of good times and bad.

Of death and divorce.

All forgotten so he could travel to the East Coast with a woman he'd been dating for three months.

One good thing, however, had come from it. His actions had been the catalyst Iris needed to do something more with her life other than work for her best friend.

Former best friend.

Six years working for Dash was long enough.

The job paid well, but being his housekeeper, cook, and errand runner wasn't her dream career.

She'd pushed what she wanted aside because Dash needed her, and she'd needed him, so she built her world around him.

So not healthy.

Iris had realized something else at his party on New Year's Eve. Once he married—Raina or some other woman—Iris would find herself out of a job. No one wanted their husband's female so-called bestie living in the backyard and running their household. That was when she finally realized their friends-forever deal could never last.

She'd put off her dreams long enough.

It was time to do something.

To make a change.

A big one.

Not for anyone else.

But for herself.

She wanted to be a chef and have a family.

That would never happen if she stayed.

As she considered the possibilities, excitement shot to the tips of her toes. Quitting her job was the first step to making her dreams come true.

Only Henry knew of her plans.

She would tell Dash after she found an apartment. Well, another one. She'd signed the lease on the perfect place, walking distance to the culinary school and within her price range. Her move-in date had been scheduled. Unfortunately two days ago, severe water damage to two units, including her future one, meant she'd received her deposit back and needed to find a new place to live since there were no other vacancies.

A knock sounded.

She stood and padded across the hardwood floor in llama slipper socks—a Christmas present from Audra, Blaise and Hadley's niece.

As Iris opened the door, cold air surrounded her. Despite her long-sleeved shirt and leggings, goose bumps covered her skin. She shivered.

"You're cold." Henry was six feet tall and the definition of handsome with light brown hair, hazel-green eyes, and a killer smile. He dressed to impress with an occasional clothing choice meant to shock others. Tonight, he wore a sweater with a pair of plaid pants. "I'll warm you up."

Someone cleared his throat.

Iris peered around Henry.

Frowning, Dash stood on the stone path with his arms crossed. He had light brown hair like Henry, but the similarities ended there. Dash was four inches taller and wore whatever clothes Iris laid out for him. Tonight was a forest green long-sleeved T-shirt and jeans. He always changed as soon as he arrived home from work.

"What are you doing here?" she asked him. He hadn't been to the cottage in over two months. November seventh was the last time if she wanted to get technical, which she didn't. "Is everything okay?"

Lines creased his forehead. He started to speak and then stopped himself.

That was…odd.

Though he often spoke without thinking, there was a reason. His brilliant brain ran at lightspeed which meant he appeared socially inept when really he was onto another topic before anyone else. Something must be wrong for him to clam up.

But she couldn't imagine what. Unless he'd somehow found out what she was planning to do.

Her fingers tightened around the doorknob. "Do I need to clean up the house tonight?"

"No. We're not heathens."

The sound of Henry's voice jolted her. She'd been so focused on Dash, she'd forgotten they weren't alone.

Iris turned her attention onto Henry. "You didn't see the house after the New Year's Eve party."

He laughed. "I might have contributed to that, but you'll only find glasses in the sink and empty plates and platters on the counter."

"Leave it until morning." Dash's voice was hoarse.

She hoped he wasn't coming down with something.

Henry kissed her cheek and then stepped into the cottage, pulling her with him. "You're going to catch a chill out here."

As soon as she was inside, she rubbed her hands

over her arms. "Gotta love forced air heating."

Dash entered behind them and closed the door. He went to the couch, picked up a blue fleece throw that matched his eye color, and wrapped the blanket around her shoulders. "You should wear a jacket."

"I was just opening the door." She pinned Dash with a narrowed gaze. "You never told me why you're here."

He rubbed his neck before glancing at Henry.

"Dashiell wanted to say good night," Henry answered for him.

Dash straightened as if suddenly buoyed. "That's right. And to thank you. The guys enjoyed the snacks."

Henry nodded. "The food was superb. Poker night is a waste of your talent."

Iris wanted to glare at Henry, but she couldn't with Dash nearby. "How was poker night?"

"Blaise won." Henry laughed. "Again."

Dash nodded. "The guy has the magic touch with cards."

"Or a system," Henry suggested. "Maybe he created a poker code."

Dash shrugged. "If that's the case, Blaise deserves it. He's made us all richer with his investment algorithms."

It was Henry's turn to nod.

"I wouldn't put it past Blaise." Iris was warming up, but she pulled the throw tighter around her to chase away the cold faster. "You should have seen him when we played board games on Christmas Day. When Audra beat him twice, he demanded a rematch."

The corners of Dash's mouth tipped up. "I would have paid to see that."

"Maybe this year," Henry said before Iris could reply. "Unless you go back east to be with Raina's family again."

Dash's eyes darkened to a stormy blue. "I'll be here. My parents asked me to stick around. They missed having me to fight over for the holidays."

His parents *had asked*. He didn't decide himself.
Typical.

Dash avoided conflict and confrontation. Change, too.

That was why the guys called him Mr. Status Quo.

The nickname fit, which explained why she was working hard to keep his household running the same way after she left. She'd hired three people to take her place. Once they finished their training next week, he would never know she wasn't there. To be honest, he hadn't noticed the others doing various jobs for the past week. Not that he was around much.

She glanced at the clock. "Shouldn't you be gaming now?"

His cheeks turned pink. "I will soon. After I see Henry out."

Henry rolled his eyes. "I found my way here. I

can make it back without getting lost."

"Just being a polite host." Dash shifted his weight between his feet. "It's freezing outside."

"You're a good friend to be so concerned about my well-being." Henry sounded amused. He turned his attention to Iris. "Since Dashiell feels the need to chaperone me, I'll quickly make our plans."

"Plans?" She and Dash spoke in unison.

"Yes." Henry beamed, appearing pleased at himself. "For tomorrow."

"Day or evening?" Iris had mentioned looking at apartments this weekend, but she hadn't expected him to offer to go with her.

"Both."

Dash wiped his face.

Maybe he was getting sick. Nothing else, including Raina, kept him from his Friday night gaming marathons.

"I don't want to take up your entire Saturday," she said, confused what Henry had in mind.

"Saturday, Sunday, Monday, Tuesday, etcetera," Henry spouted. "All the days are the same to me."

Oh. She remembered he didn't work. "Fine."

Dash flinched. "You're agreeing just like that?"

She nodded. "Do I need to bring anything with me?"

Henry tapped his chin.

Uh-oh. Iris recognized his mischievous expression. Henry was up to something.

"No food or passport required," he said finally.

"Passport?" Dash's Adam's apple bobbed. "Do you even have one, Iris? When was the last time you took a vacation? Traveled overseas?"

His incredulous tone angered Iris. Dash would never ask anyone else those questions. He, however, didn't believe she had a desire to do anything except work for him. As if washing clothes, cleaning house, cooking, and running errands was her life's purpose.

That burned.

But she didn't know what to say without crossing the line. He might not be her best friend any longer, but he was her boss. She blew out a breath to calm her spiraling anger.

Henry shook his head.

"I took a vacation when you were with Raina's family." Which she'd told him, explaining how she and Henry had explored a few of Portland's holiday offerings—riding the train at the Oregon Zoo to strolling through the festival of lights before listening to performers at the Grotto. But he'd most likely had something else on his mind. "It was a staycation."

Henry wrapped his arm around Iris and pulled her close against him. "I had fun with you."

"It was a blast." When she'd been growing up, her parents had been too busy working at their restaurant to do those things with her. As an adult, she hadn't had the money or time. Once she did, she hadn't wanted to go alone. She stared at Dash. "I have a passport."

Henry squeezed her. "She needs one to go to Paris for dinner or Milan for a fashion show or London to watch tennis."

Iris tried not to laugh. He did those things on his dates, but she wasn't sure why he was telling Dash. Henry was the only unattached billionaire she knew, but he would never do any of those things with her. They were nothing more than friends. Still, she appreciated his support. She only wished she didn't need it.

She raised her chin. "Or the opera in San Francisco."

Henry winked. "Or a Broadway musical in the Big Apple."

The funny thing was, if Iris wanted to do those things, Henry would take her. As a friend or a plus-one. It wouldn't matter to him. He enjoyed having fun and the more outlandish the activity the better.

Dash, however, turned down her suggestions to go to the movies or hiking or a restaurant, so she'd stopped asking. They no longer ate meals together at the house. Something they used to do whenever they could.

She'd been so blind. Their friendship had become completely lopsided. The realization saddened her but provided more proof she needed to move on and follow her own path.

Iris focused on Henry, not knowing what kind of game he was playing tonight, but she would go along with it for now. "How should I dress tomorrow?"

"Warm because we'll be in and out."

Dash's gaze bounced between her and Henry, but his expression revealed nothing that he might be feeling.

"I can do that." A mix of rain and snow was expected, but she'd been born and raised in Portland. An umbrella wasn't necessary. "What time?"

Henry tilted his head as if contemplating one of life's greatest questions. "I don't wake up until eleven, so let's say noon."

"What about my lunch?" Dash asked.

Really? That was what he wanted to know?

She inhaled and then exhaled slowly. "Saturday is my day off. I'll leave a plate for you in the refrigerator the way I always do."

His jawline tensed. "If it's easier for you, I can grab something myself."

"Well, isn't that nice of you to offer?" Henry didn't sound pleased at all. "I'm sure Raina will bring you lunch if you ask her."

"She's at a bachelorette weekend." Dash's words rushed out.

That was the first Iris had heard about that. No wonder he'd hosted poker night and was worried about lunch. Still, that wasn't her problem.

"I hope you're not missing your girlfriend too much." Henry pulled Iris closer and brushed his lips over her hair. "I'm looking forward to tomorrow."

Dash's face hardened. His nostrils flared.

"Is there a problem?" Henry asked.

"No." Dash's balled fist told another story. He must miss Raina.

Not surprising. The two spent much of his free time together.

"Is there anything you need me for this weekend?" Iris made his meals, but she had the weekends to herself unless he was entertaining or one of his friends hired her to cater a party.

"Other than the usual, no," Dash said. "Ready to go, Henry?"

Henry kept his arm around her. "What makes you think I'm leaving?"

Dash rocked back on the heels of his tennis shoes. "Iris is tired."

At least he noticed that. She nodded. "I am."

"Then you should sleep." Henry let go of her. "We have tomorrow to talk."

"Yes." Because she didn't want Dash around when they spoke. "If you're running late, let me know."

"I will." Henry kissed her forehead. "Sweet dreams tonight. You'll be living one tomorrow."

Iris laughed. Henry should write a book with all his lines. "Can't wait."

Dash shook his head.

The guy looked like he needed a hug, but that was Raina's job now. "Good night, Dash."

The two men left, closing the door behind them.

That had been weird. Dash wasn't acting normal, and Henry was up to something. The question was what? And how did she fit into it?

Chapter Three

Saturday night, Dash paced in front of his bedroom windows, forcing himself not to peek at the backyard. Even if he did, he couldn't see if Iris was home yet. He knew that—had known that before tonight—but he'd peered out from the various rooms on this side of the second floor as if to convince himself that was true. He'd also gone to the cottage—twice—but no lights had been on inside.

Stupid.

What was wrong with him? He was turning into a stalker. What Iris did in her free time was her own business.

Just friends.

Dash kept telling himself that. Except…

He couldn't stop thinking about Iris and Henry

being together.

Why hadn't Dash spoken to her about it on January first? The same reason he ended up spending Christmas with Raina and her family—not making waves was easiest.

Dash didn't do drama. Arguing, confrontation, fighting—forget about it. Yet, with Iris…

Years ago, they'd made a deal to be friends forever.

After an almost kiss.

His idea.

One that had burst from his lips out of fear of losing the person he needed in his chaotic life at the time.

Rubbing his thumb over his fingertips, he made another lap. His agitation kept building, spiraling until he wanted to yell. He could. No one would hear him in this huge house. But he had a feeling nothing would ease his tension except seeing that Iris was okay. More than that, smiling and happy.

As if he could make her appear faster, he quickened his steps in front of the windows.

The frustration gnawing at him was new. He kept his cool unless a project was way behind schedule, people were being jerks, or his friends acting just plain dumb—like Blaise and Wes with the women they loved.

Idiots.

Six years ago, Iris had caused Dash to feel this

troubled. Not her exactly, her lousy excuse for a father. The guy had met a younger woman online, sold the family restaurant and with it the apartment above it they'd called home, and moved out of state to be closer to his girlfriend, leaving his daughter unemployed and homeless three months after the death of her mother.

Dash had stepped up then. It was time for him to do it again and make sure she didn't end up brokenhearted over Henry. That was what friends did for each other.

Henry might be self-absorbed, but he was a good friend, too. He made a difference with his philanthropic endeavors. Still, he wasn't good enough for Iris.

Which was why Dash needed to say something to her before it was too late.

Unless it already was.

Dash tugged at the collar of his long-sleeved T-shirt. That didn't help.

Normally, silence didn't bother him, but maybe the quiet was getting to him. He'd turned on music earlier. He'd also worked, watched TV, and played a new game. Nothing took his mind off Iris.

A glance at the clock told him only two minutes had passed since the last time he checked. A quarter after ten wasn't late for a Saturday night, but he wanted to know where she was.

For months, his friends had been beta testing a

GPS tracking device for Dash. He hadn't given one to Iris. She'd never been threatened or needed security. Henry, however, had one.

Temptation flared, burning a hole in Dash's gut. *Nope.*

He wouldn't turn into a total creeper and log on to the tracking app to see where Henry was. So what if Iris had left at a quarter past twelve, almost ten hours ago? She would be home soon. She had to be. Unless…

What if she wasn't coming home tonight?

Dash sucked in a breath. He didn't want to know the answer.

Except he really did.

Ugh. Strange and unfamiliar emotions swirled inside him.

Why had this become such a big deal?

Iris dated. Didn't she? Maybe not. He had no idea what she did on her time off. He couldn't remember hearing any guys' names, not that he'd asked, or recall checking to see if she'd stayed out all night. It didn't matter because she was always around when he needed her the next day. Yet, tonight…

His phone rang.

The ringtone was the Main Theme from the Ori and the Blind Forest video game.

Not Iris, but Raina.

He snagged the phone from his pocket. "Hey. Having a good time?"

"Hi, babe." She spoke with affection. "I'm having a fantastic weekend. So glad you talked me into coming. We're getting ready to go dancing."

Dash wasn't much of a dancer, but he'd tried his best for Raina's sake at Blaise and Hadley's wedding. He'd be doing the same when Wes and Paige set a date for their nuptials. "Sounds fun."

"It will be." Laughter sounded in the background. Someone yelled tequila shots. "No deadlines to worry about. Lots of girl talk. A relaxing spa day. This trip is exactly what I needed."

"You've been working hard." Multiple issues had delayed her newest game's launch. That had meant extra hours during the week and on weekends. She'd almost had to cancel on her friend's bachelorette party, but he'd convinced her to go even though she'd be playing catch-up once she returned. "You deserve some R and R."

"I wish you were with me."

He laughed. "Not sure I would enjoy the spa and girl talk as much as you."

Raina sighed. "The massage was heavenly."

"That part would be awesome. Maybe I should make an appointment." He hadn't had one in over a week. He rolled his shoulders. "My muscles are tight."

"Higher workload?"

"Not really." Though maybe his job was why his stress level kept skyrocketing today.

"Anything I can do?" she asked.

"Keep enjoying yourself so you're all smiles when you come home."

"I will. Oh, before I forget." Raina paused. "What's going on with Henry and Iris?"

Hearing the two names together sent Dash's stomach plummeting. "What do you mean?"

"Henry posted a pic of him and Iris together on his IG."

A band tightened around Dash's chest. Squeezed. Tight. He forced himself to breathe. "What did the caption say?"

"Having fun in the rain. No hashtag 'official' or anything like that."

He released the breath he'd been holding. "They had plans to hang out today."

"Are they dating?" Curiosity dripped from each word.

Nausea set in. "No idea, but Henry is anti-commitment. If something is going on, I hope he doesn't hurt Iris."

"I thought the kisses on New Year's Eve were them joking around, but she's an adult. She can handle it."

"Yes." She'd been nineteen when she left culinary school to care for her mother, who'd had ALS and died three years later. Iris had grown up fast. She'd had no other choice. "But being with Henry is like winning an all-expenses paid vacation to a theme park where fun is the priority. It isn't reality."

"True." Another pause. "Maybe he's trying to hire Iris away from you."

Dash swallowed around the lump in his throat. Blaise kept teasing he would do that. So had the others. Could that be why Henry wanted to spend more time with her?

Thinking Henry's interest was about Iris's skills and work ethic didn't bring any relief. Dash remembered the items out of place in the pantry. The space had been clean and organized, as usual, but a few things weren't where they belonged. That was unlike Iris. Was that connected to her being with Henry?

"Maybe," Dash said.

"That must be it," Raina said in a matter-of-fact tone. "Iris is a sweetheart, but Henry Davenport could do so much better for a girlfriend than a housekeeper with only a high school diploma."

Dash's jaw tensed. He'd never heard Raina talk that way, and he didn't like it. Especially about Iris. "Henry would be fortunate to date Iris."

Even if Dash wouldn't like it.

"But Henry is…Henry." Raina laughed. "The women he goes out with—"

"Iris is smart, honest, and hardworking." Plus, her smile lit up a room and her eyes shone with kindness. "Not to mention my best friend. And don't forget, I dropped out of college before my junior year, so I only have a high school diploma, too."

"You don't need a degree. You founded a company in your freshman dorm room. Everyone knows you're brilliant."

"So is Iris."

"You're so loyal. That's something I love about you." Raina made a kissing sound. "You and Iris were besties growing up, but you have to admit, she's more of an employee now."

"She's both." The words flew out of his mouth.

"Oh, sweetie. Iris is a wonderful cook and housekeeper. She does an excellent job, but when was the last time you did anything with her outside of the house?"

Raina's voice held no challenge, but Dash went on the defensive. "We…"

He thought back to the past three months. Then six. A year.

Not one thing came to mind.

The year before that, either.

Dash tried to remember something these past three years but couldn't. He slumped. "We do things at the house."

Like chatting while she cooked or spending Christmas Day together.

Except they hadn't done that this year, either.

Unease slithered through him.

Did Iris think of him as only her employer now? What about them being friends forever?

Not knowing the answers to those questions sucked.

"We're heading out," Raina said, interrupting his thoughts.

"Enjoy yourself."

"I will." She sounded as if she were smiling. "Bye, babe."

The line disconnected before he said goodbye. Not a problem. He would see Raina next weekend. His week was full, but she would text him when she arrived home, if not sooner.

The side gate slammed.

Dash straightened. That was the entrance Iris used to get to the cottage.

She was home.

Finally.

He ran down the stairs, taking two at a time, and out into the backyard. The night air stung his lungs, but he wasn't cold in his sweats and hoodie. Who was he kidding? He would put up with freezing rain if that meant he could see Iris.

Talk to her.

Warn her off Henry.

He hurried along the stone path.

Iris stood at the cottage's front door. The porch light cast shadows on her face. She wore a red parka, gray striped beanie, jeans, and snow boots. Puffs of her breath hung on the air. Her keys jingled in her gloved hand.

Dash came closer. "Iris."

She glanced his way. Her keys fell on to the

doormat. "Oops."

He stepped forward. "I didn't mean to startle you."

Or scare you.

Dash dragged his hand through his hair. He didn't want to say the wrong thing. Though if anyone knew him—his strengths and his flaws—Iris did. "Sorry."

"It's okay." She picked up the keys. "Just not used to seeing you over here."

Especially two nights in a row.

His fault.

Again.

He used to spend time at the cottage playing video games and talking to her. It was the perfect place for downtime. Why had they stopped? If there was a reason, he didn't remember it.

"Can I come in?" he asked.

"Sure." Iris inserted the key into the lock before glancing his way with an unreadable expression on her face. "You okay?"

Her concern made him shift uncomfortably. Dash wished he was okay, but his palms sweated. He rubbed them over his sweatpants. "I will be."

After he spoke with her, he would feel better. At least, he hoped so.

They went inside where it was dark, and Dash closed the door behind him.

Warmth enveloped him.

A light turned on.

He blinked.

"It's warm and cozy in here." He tried to sound nonchalant but was unsure if he succeeded. "Mind if I sit?"

Motioning to the love seat, she removed her gloves, hat, and coat. Her cheeks were flushed from the cold. Her hair was messy from her beanie. She wore a fuzzy purple sweater that barely covered her jeans' waistband.

The sweater looked good on her, but it wasn't designed to keep her warm. "Did you get cold?"

"I'm fine."

"I meant when you were out earlier. With Henry." The final word tasted like sand in Dash's mouth.

She sat on an overstuffed chair where she enjoyed reading. At least, she used to read there. "No. We stayed warm."

That didn't tell him much. As all the ways she and Henry could stay warm together streamed through Dash's mind, he rubbed the back of his tight neck. "How was your day?"

Her shoulders sagged. "Frustrating."

Dash bolted forward. "Did Henry—"

"He made everything better."

Of course he did because that was what Henry did. The guy had once handed out hundred-dollar bills to strangers in downtown Portland. The reason? Henry enjoyed seeing people smile after the unexpected gift.

Iris leaned forward in the chair. "What's going on?"

He shifted uncomfortably. "This is harder than I thought it would be."

Her brows drew together. She stood, came over to the love seat, and sat next to him. "What?"

"Are you…" The words froze on Dash's lips. He wiped his hands on his sweatpants again.

"We've been through so much over the years with your parents and mine." Iris placed her hand over his. Her skin was soft but cold from her being outside. Still, her touch comforted him. "You can tell me anything."

"I know."

Dash did. No matter what Raina might think, Iris was his best friend. She always would be. No one knew him better, which was why he shouldn't be acting like they were thirteen again and he was the geeky new kid too nervous to speak to the prettiest girl at school when she'd introduced herself on his first day. They'd been inseparable, through good times and bad, ever since.

"Are you and Henry…" Serious? No, that wasn't the right word when Dash didn't know what was going on. He would go with the more obvious term. "Dating?"

Her lips parted. She raised her hand off his. "Me and Henry?"

Dash nodded.

She laughed. "Where did you get that crazy idea?"

The band around his chest loosened so he could breathe easier. "You went out today."

Iris's mouth slanted. "You spend time with Henry, and you're not dating him."

"We're friends, but I don't greet him with a kiss."

"That's just Henry." The tip of her pink tongue darted out and ran across her upper lip. "He loves women no matter the age or who they are."

"What about when you kissed him on New Year's Eve?"

She hesitated. "Henry had his reason for the kiss. None of which had to do with me."

"So you and Henry…"

"Are friends. Nothing more," she finished for Dash. "Henry's kind and generous, but he'll be the first to admit he isn't boyfriend material. I listen when a guy says something like that."

"Good." Tension melted from Dash. "I didn't want him to hurt you."

"Thanks, but please give me a little credit. I can take care of myself."

"That's what Raina said."

Iris stiffened. "You spoke to Raina about this?"

"She asked about the selfie Henry posted today."

"Henry posts lots of selfies. His DNA requires him to be the center of attention, and he enjoys keeping people guessing. Whether in person or on social media."

True. Everything Iris said made sense. But Dash still wanted to ask. "So this is just Henry…"

"Being Henry," she said without missing a beat. "Who knows what motivates him?"

"Other than his goddaughter."

"His friends and those in need, too," she added with a grin.

Guess Iris knew Henry pretty well. The realization stung because Dash wanted to keep her for himself. "So what did you do today?"

As Iris's face paled, her smile vanished. She bit her lower lip, something she did whenever she was nervous or…procrastinating.

Uh-oh. This didn't look good. "Hey, like you told me, you can tell me anything. We're best friends."

She shot him a look of disbelief. "We *were* best friends."

Her use of past tense drove home how much he'd taken Iris for granted. He slouched, the weight of what he'd done making it impossible to think or sit straight.

What had he done?

Or in her case, not done.

Since Iris moved in with him six years ago, he'd built strong friendships with Adam, Blaise, Brett, Henry, Kieran, Mason, and Wes. They became brothers. As they'd built a family of choice, Dash had allowed his most important friendship to flounder. The fact it was happening had never entered his mind.

Not once.

And she should have been the priority because…

He was hers.

Iris had always taken care of him. Even when they were teenagers.

Now, she worked without complaining. Not once had she claimed to feel bad. If she'd been sick, she'd never told him, and he… He hadn't noticed. She'd never asked him for anything, not even days off.

What was wrong with him?

Dash forced the employees at his company to use their vacation time. Everyone needed a break, time off to recharge, but he never thought of doing that with Iris.

Six years.

Six years with only her regular days off except for her staycation while he was away over the holidays.

That was…

Unforgivable.

He'd believed Christmas had been the first time he'd let her down. That had only been one in a series of mistakes. Not small ones, enormous fill-him-with-regret mistakes. He hadn't acted like a best friend. He hadn't even been a good boss.

Ashamed, he scrubbed his face with his hand.

"Anyway," she continued. "I appreciate everything you've done for me, but…"

His breath caught in his throat. He must have missed what she'd said.

Way to go, Cabot.

He forced himself not to interrupt and apologize. Those were just words, however heartfelt, when his actions for years would contradict them.

This was her time to talk. Not his.

She rubbed her eyes. "I've been putting off telling you something. I can't wait any longer."

Dash wanted to put her at ease. "Whatever you have to say won't change anything."

Her gaze, full of compassion, met his. "I'm doing what I can so nothing will change for you."

"I appreciate that." Even if he had no idea what she was talking about. It didn't matter. Whatever she said, they would move on so he could make up for neglecting their friendship.

Unless...

Dash's heartbeat roared in his ears. What if it was too late? What if she no longer wanted him in her life?

Chapter Four

On the couch next to Dash, Iris drew her knees to her chest and wrapped her arms around her legs. Quitting would hit him hard, which was why she'd been waiting for the right time to tell him. Tonight wasn't it.

The apartment search had drained her. Twice, she and Henry had arrived at a place only to find someone turned in an application minutes earlier. Sure, she could do the same which Iris had, but she hated being next in line if the first applicant fell through.

Talk about frustrating.

But she hadn't given up. They looked at other apartments. Only those had been too expensive or too run-down. One building had been in such bad shape she'd told Henry's chauffeur, Frank, not to stop.

With less than a week to find a place and move, she couldn't stop worrying. Having nowhere to live brought back memories of finding herself jobless and homeless when her father sold their restaurant. If only that had been the worst thing he did…

She inhaled deeply to slow her racing pulse.

This time, however, was different.

Iris didn't need to rely on anyone but herself. Granted, she'd used over a third of her bonus to pay the culinary school tuition. But she also had a credit card, a savings account, and a Roth IRA. None of which she had when she was twenty-two. Worse comes to worst, she could move into a short-term rental or a room somewhere until an apartment opened up. She had enough money to live on while she was in school and for three months after that.

No reason to panic.

I will find a place tomorrow.

"Iris?" Concern filled Dash's voice. He stood and paced in front of the coffee table. "Please talk to me."

Dash had been manipulated by his parents, so he didn't play games with others. He was open, honest, and for a twenty-eight-year-old billionaire, a tad naïve. Those things made him who he was—a nice guy.

She might not have the same IQ as him, but she wasn't stupid. There wouldn't be a good time to tell him, no matter how hard she'd been wishing otherwise. She should have given her two-week notice last weekend. She hadn't, so she had to do it now.

Iris shivered. "Give me a minute."

"Take all the time you need." His tense jaw contradicted his words, but he attempted a smile. A half-hearted one with no teeth showing. "I'm going to grab a soda."

"I don't have any." She didn't drink the stuff—too sweet—but she used to keep cans on hand for Dash until he stopped dropping by. "There's iced tea and flavored water."

"Oh, okay." His brow wrinkled, something it did when he was thinking. "Want anything?"

"No, thanks."

Shoulders hunched slightly, he went around the corner to the kitchen.

Iris hated seeing him hurting, but she wasn't doing it on purpose. Things weren't the same between them. For whatever reason, Dash hadn't noticed, or he'd ignored it. Bottom line, they weren't as close as they'd once been. That wasn't an observation, but a fact and why she'd said they *were* best friends.

Not *currently* best friends.

They shared the blame for that happening. He hadn't made their friendship a priority, and she'd thought doing everything for him would be enough to save it.

"Are you sure you don't want something?" Dash called out.

Her stomach churned. Drinking or eating anything wouldn't be smart. She pulled her legs in closer. "I'm good."

And she was.

Maybe not at this moment, but overall, she was more excited about her future than she'd been in a long time.

Iris had always gone along with whatever Dash wanted. She hadn't spoken up about anything over the years, including them not spending time together.

Friends forever.

Except their deal had been nothing more than an excuse.

She'd continued to work hard and kept pretending being his housekeeper was enough. A potent combination of fear and lack of self-confidence kept her doing anything else. Every time a dream surfaced, she buried it deep again. She'd put Dash first, never realizing her needs mattered, too.

Not until spending time with Henry over Christmas.

A mashup of a fairy godfather and psychologist, he listened to her and asked questions that no one, including Dash, had ever thought to ask. Talking to Henry opened a spill-gate of her hopes and dreams she hadn't wanted to close.

She'd allowed herself to get stuck. Some of that was because of gratitude to Dash, but she was the biggest problem. Iris could no longer settle because she was afraid of failing or being abandoned. Finding herself alone wasn't the worst thing that could happen.

Truth was, she was on her own.

Why not go after what she wanted?

Which was what Iris was going to do. She didn't hate her job, but she wanted…more. Things she couldn't have if she continued working for Dash.

A kitchen cabinet closed. He must be pouring his drink into a glass. Funny, but she remembered when they were in high school and he drank straight from the jug. That had bugged his mom. "Habit" had been his reply.

Not much had changed.

"You got any cookies?" he asked.

"In the jar on the counter."

"Store-bought?"

"Homemade." Which he should know. The fact he asked drove home how much they'd grown apart.

Iris cared about Dash. She always would.

Once upon a time, she fancied herself in love with him. A crush, Iris realized later, but gorgeous geeks were her type, which was why she'd introduced herself as soon as she saw him the first day of school so many years ago. Finding herself parked in Dash's friend zone had hurt—oh, the tears and belief she'd never get over her broken heart—but it had been for the best.

"Want one?" Dash asked.

"No, but help yourself."

Their friendship had been the most important thing in her life, which was part of why she'd fallen for him, but she'd kept her feelings a secret. One reason had been their friends-forever deal. Funny how something like that could define her life. The other reason was because she wanted something Dash couldn't give her—love.

Iris wanted the happily ever after—marriage, kids, animals. Then and now, she dreamed of having a family of her own. Someday, she would find the right man who would love her, treat her as an equal, and make her a priority the way she would with him.

Dash dated when it was convenient and didn't get in his way. His divorced parents' tug-of-war, wanting him to pick a side, making him the prize where there could be no winner, had colored his view of love. He didn't believe love lasted, if it existed at all. No one would call him a romantic. Iris took care of everything for his dates. She picked out gifts, sent flowers in his name, and made dinner reservations.

If any of the women had figured this out, Dash had never mentioned it to her. But perhaps none cared, if they had known. Dash dated easygoing women who let him do what he wanted, until they tired of waiting for things to move to the next level.

A level that would never happen if Dash had a choice.

Raina, however, appeared to have more patience

than the others. Maybe she was in this for the long haul, not just a few months. If so, Iris wished the woman luck. Unlike the other five guys who'd gotten engaged—and in four cases, married—quickly, Dash Cabot would never do that.

He claimed he never wanted to get married.

That made Dash a shoo-in to win the bet. She'd known from the beginning he would be the last single man standing, whether or not he tried, because he wasn't the marrying kind.

With a glass of water in hand, he returned. "I didn't eat all the cookies. Figured you might want one later."

She lowered her feet to the floor and tried to find a comfortable position. Their talk might take a while. "So you left one?"

"Two." He sat before taking a sip.

Iris inhaled and then exhaled slowly.

A corner of Dash's mouth curved upward. "I can hear the gears in your brain from here."

"They're cranking," she joked, hoping to put herself at ease.

It didn't.

He set his glass on the table. "What's going on?"

Might as well get this over with. "I've enrolled in culinary school."

Dash's jaw relaxed. His eyes brightened. "Another weekend workshop?"

Iris had taken those in the past with his full

support, though she'd turned down his offer to pay for the classes. "No, I'll be a full-time student."

He opened his mouth and then closed it. A range of emotions crossed his face—confusion, surprise, anger.

"That's not possible." His voice was tight as if he were trying to rein himself in. "You work for me full-time."

She angled toward him. "You've done so much for me, Dash. I'll never be able to thank you for taking me in when I had nowhere else to go and giving me a job. I've enjoyed working for you, but my dream has always been to be a chef. That got put on hold when my mom needed me, but now…"

"Now what?" Deep lines formed on his forehead and around his mouth. "Are you leaving me?"

His words came out raw and harsh.

Her breath hitched. A band appeared to wrap around her chest, squeezing tightly.

Dash had never sounded that way before. Not even during the worst times with his parents. But she needed to continue. "Yes. I'm resigning as your housekeeper."

He jumped to his feet. Mumbled to himself. Paced in front of the coffee table.

"You're more than a housekeeper." The words flew out. "You cook and run errands. You shop for my clothes and tell me what to wear. You keep my personal life on track."

If he'd been sitting next to her, she would have reached out to him. But maybe it was better this way. He would need to learn to settle himself without her help. "Others will do those things for you."

"No." He stopped pacing. His hands balled before he flexed his fingers. "I want you to do them. The way you always have. You can't leave. We'll find a way for you to go to school and stay with me."

Normally, she gave in to him. That tendency had her wanting to do just that. Not this time. She couldn't.

Iris pressed her shoulders back. "This isn't what you expected, and I'm sorry for upsetting you, but you'll get used to the change sooner than you think. I hired people. I've been training them this past week."

He shook his head. "That explains the pantry."

"What?"

"Nothing." Dash stared at her, a muscle ticking at his jaw. "I had no idea you weren't happy. Name your salary. Whatever it is you want, I'll pay it."

Of course he would because he had enough money to last a hundred lifetimes. He wouldn't miss a million or even ten million dollars.

"I don't want your money. You pay me way more than you should."

"Then tell me what will make you happier."

"I'm not unhappy, Dash." She wanted him to see this from her side, not his. "My plan was always to finish the culinary school program. I didn't have the money to do that after my mom died, so I've been saving since then. Thanks to your Christmas bonus, I no longer have to wait."

"Christmas bonus, huh?" Dash's nostrils flared. "When do classes start?"

"A week from Monday. I'm sorry for not telling you sooner. That's on me for not giving two weeks' notice."

Mumbling again, he glanced up at the ceiling. "I don't care about that. I don't want you to leave."

"The new staff are skilled. They're super nice. You won't know I'm gone."

His face reddened. "How can you say that? You've been taking care of me, my apartment, and then this house for six years. You're irreplaceable. And not only for what you do. You belong here. We're friends."

"We don't see much of each other these days." And even less now that he was dating Raina.

"But I like knowing you're around." He paced again, moving his arms in front of him as if he were having a conversation in his head. "Tell me what I can do to change your mind."

"Nothing." She didn't hesitate to answer. "This isn't about you or the job. It's about me. My mom's illness derailed my plans when I was nineteen. Then my dad's midlife crisis three years later made me put off what I wanted to do again. I'm almost twenty-nine. It's time to go back. Thank you for giving me this opportunity."

"But—"

"It'll all work out."

"No, it won't." Dash sat on the love seat, his shoulders slumping. He dragged his hand through his hair. Light brown strands stuck up, making him look rumpled. If not for his frown, she'd call him adorable, too. "Please don't do this. I'm begging you."

"I hired the best people for you." She wanted to convince him he would be okay. "Janice and Leo Peabody will handle the house. They'll also manage the lawn and maintenance crew. Leo is a trained butler. Janice is a housekeeper. Tony Chivas will be your personal chef. We were classmates at culinary school, and we've kept in touch over the years. He's worked at a variety of places since then but was looking for a position without the crazy hours a restaurant entails."

Dash's gaze narrowed. "You hired three people to take your place?"

She nodded. "I couldn't find one person to do it all. Janice and Leo are like getting a two-for-one deal. They are moving into the cottage on Friday."

Dash's jaw dropped. His face hardened. "You are not moving out."

Iris flinched. She wasn't used to him raising his voice. "I can't stay here if I'm not working for you."

"This is your home." His voice softened a little. "You're staying."

His earnest tone tugged at her heart. Iris blew out a breath. "I love this cottage and your estate. I'll never forget helping you pick out this place, but it's time for me to move on. I don't own a car, and I'd rather not have to buy one right now, so I'm hoping to find an apartment that's close to school."

"Wait." He straightened. "You don't have an apartment yet?"

"I put a deposit on a place, but it fell through," she admitted. "Henry took me out today to look at a few apartments, and I plan to go out again tomorrow."

Dash's lips parted. "Henry knows you're returning to culinary school?"

"Yes. He thinks it's a good idea."

Dash rolled his eyes. "Henry would because he doesn't know any better."

"Brett thinks so, too. Earlier tonight, he helped me with a budget to follow while I'm in school to make sure I don't run out of money before I graduate."

Dash stared with an expression of disbelief. "Don't go, Iris. Not having a place to live is a sign this isn't the right time. Wait another term. The fall would be better, or a year from now. I promise. We'll figure this out together."

"I've waited long enough, and I have a backup plan if I can't find another apartment."

That muscle ticked at his jaw once more. His eyes

were dark and serious. "You're one step from being homeless again."

That wasn't fair. "No, I'm not. I have savings."

"Not enough if Brett needed to help you with a budget." Dash's gaze locked on hers.

"Henry suggested I speak with Brett."

"I'll help you. Whatever you need." Dash's voice was hoarse, unnatural. "Just…stay."

"I can't." She'd expected him to be upset but not to push back like this. "This is my dream, Dash. You were so excited and nervous when you started your company. That's how I feel now."

"I need you." His voice cracked. His eyes gleamed. "You've been the one constant in my life for the past fifteen years."

"Twelve," she corrected softly. "The last three haven't been the same."

"I messed up. I know that. And I'm sorry." His gaze implored her. "I'll make it up to you. I can't lose you, Iris."

"Oh, Dash." She held his hand and squeezed. "You're not losing me. I'll still be in Portland."

"We'll never see each other."

"We don't now." She wasn't being flippant, just honest. "You work, go out with Raina, see the guys, and play your video games. We hardly eat meals together or bump into each other these days."

"Raina—"

"There were others before her." Iris kept her

voice steady and calm. She didn't want to upset Dash more, but she needed him to see things how they were. Not how he thought or wanted them to be. "And you've become closer to others."

You don't need me the way you did was implied but unspoken.

He nodded once before seeming to catch himself. "I want to spend time with you."

"You have my number." Which he used to text her, never call. Dash wasn't one for talking on the phone.

"I'm sorry."

"You have nothing to be sorry about." Iris meant that. "I know this isn't what you want, but I'm ready to see what comes next."

"I didn't mean…" He rubbed the back of his neck again. "We had a deal, but I let you down. I knew you'd be around, so I didn't put much effort into our friendship. And at Christmas…"

She patted his hand. "Don't be sorry. I wasn't ready to do this before. Now, I am."

"You may be ready, but I'm not. Please tell me what you need."

She'd never asked Dash for anything because she didn't want him to think she was like his parents, who always wanted money. This year was the first time she'd cashed one of his bonus checks. Henry had told her that she deserved it and could use the money to follow her dreams.

"Nothing," she said finally. "But thanks."

He wiped his eyes.

"It's going to be okay," she added.

"None of this is okay." He spoke so softly she could barely hear him. "I didn't mean to hold you back."

She scooted closer to him. "You didn't. I was where I needed to be."

Regret clouded his gaze. "How did we go from best friends to…this?"

"You founded a successful startup and were a billionaire at twenty-three. Your life changed. My job was to make sure you didn't have to worry about anything outside of work. I took care of everything so you could focus on your company. I did that because I wanted to. Not because you forced me to. But now it's time for me to do something else."

He looked away. "I hate this."

Dash would. But he wouldn't be sad for long. "Change is hard, but I hope you understand why I'm leaving."

Iris had no regrets for the decisions she'd made over the years, but as much as people teased Dash about being Mr. Status Quo, she'd been doing the same thing. It was time to embrace change and see what possibilities lay ahead.

Dash had made his dreams come true. Now, it was her turn.

Chapter Five

What was he going to do?

Dash trudged from the cottage, following the lighted pathway that would lead to a patio and his back door. The temperature had dropped, but he didn't care. The hot blood pulsing through his veins heated him enough. The night air against his face and hands cooled him. Maybe that would help him settle and stop his insides from imploding.

It felt as if a black hole had opened in his chest, pulling everything, including his heart, into it. Only regret would remain.

Heavy, gross regret.

He should have never come to the cottage tonight and lost his temper.

Dash had yelled at Iris—something he swore he

would never do after hearing his parents' shouting matches over the years—but he hadn't been able to control himself in that moment. Sure, he settled himself, lowering his voice, but he shouldn't have reacted that way. Even if she'd caught him off guard.

I'm resigning as your housekeeper.

Her words echoed in his mind. All he wanted to do was hold on to Iris and never let go. Except she wanted to go. She wanted to leave him.

He had to change her mind.

Okay, Dash hadn't been the greatest friend. He would own up to his failure there, but he hadn't ignored her completely. He made sure she had everything she needed—a place to live, food to eat, and a car to drive. Sure, she bought and cooked the food, but she hadn't had to pay for anything.

Didn't that count for something?

Yes, he'd taken her for granted, both as a friend and as an employee. She'd told him her dreams about becoming a chef when they were teenagers. Tonight, she'd left out the part of her dream where she took over her parents' restaurant, but that building belonged to someone else now.

If that part of her dream had changed, why couldn't the rest?

Dash wanted to be understanding and he was trying, but the thought of her moving out of the cottage and no longer working for him sliced into him like a light saber, bringing about another round of pain and remorse. But it also gave him an idea.

Iris was his chef. She didn't need to return to culinary school to make the title official. What she needed was…

A trip to Tuscany.

Iris loved Italian food. She had a passport and vacation time. Attending a cooking class there might sway her. A week or two away from him was better than…forever.

He entered the house and plodded up the stairs to his bedroom. Except…

Trying to bribe her to stay was being selfish. No question about it.

Asking her to stay hadn't worked. Still, he wasn't letting her go without—not a fight—trying to convince her that she was better off here than anywhere else.

He kicked off his shoes before plopping on his bed.

This wasn't only about getting what he wanted.

Dash worried about Iris moving out. She'd gone from her parents' house to his apartment. She'd never lived on her own. The cottage was part of his estate. The yard and maintenance crew were around more often than not. If Iris moved, who would be there if she needed something? Got sick or hurt? Wanted company?

Pressure built at his temples. He glanced at his pillow. Sleep might help, but he wasn't tired. Not when he had to find a way where both of them could get what they wanted.

How hard could that be?

He'd made billions with his data mining programs. People claimed he could figure out a solution to anything. None, however, was as important as this…as Iris. Surely, he could think of something.

But the next morning, after two hours' sleep, he still had nothing beyond bigger and better bribes. That sucked.

Maybe a shower would help.

After he dried off, Dash put on sweats and a hoodie. Iris never left him clothes to wear on the weekends, but during the week…

Thinking she wouldn't be doing that for him much longer hit like a punch to the gut. Dash stumbled back until his legs hit the bed. He fell on the mattress.

No way could he figure this out on his own. He needed help—someone who could analyze the situation without being so emotionally involved and tell him how to keep Iris from leaving.

Dash knew who to ask. He created a new group chat, one that excluded Henry and Brett. By not telling Dash what Iris was planning, they were part of the problem. No way would he let them know what he was doing. He typed a message and hit send. Now all he had to do was wait to see if anyone was free.

Dash: *I know we're watching football later, but is anyone available to get together earlier?*
Blaise: *Let me ask Hadley.*
Mason: *Brunch date, dude.*
Kieran: *I'm free.*
Adam: *Still in bed.*
Wes: *What do you need?*
Dash: *Iris quit.*

As Dash waited for a response, three dots appeared on his screen. Someone was replying. He breathed a sigh of relief because he needed input. He also didn't want to be alone.

Wes: *Come over anytime. I have food for the game, but I'll see what I can serve for breakfast. Coffee is brewing. Have whiskey, too, if you need it.*
Kieran: *I'll head over to Wes's and stop by Voodoo on the way.*
Blaise: *I'll be there shortly.*
Adam: *Just need to shower. Then I'll be there.*
Mason: *I'll cancel brunch and pick up bagels.*
Adam: *You okay to drive, Dash?*
Dash: *Yeah.*
Wes: *See you soon.*

Thirty minutes later, Dash drove to meet his friends. The overcast sky matched his mood. The only thing missing? A torrential downpour. But given this was winter in the Pacific Northwest, rain could happen anytime. Maybe if it poured, Iris wouldn't look at more apartments today.

Too bad he hadn't invented a way to control the weather.

Maybe he should add that to his future-projects list.

He parked and waved to his security team in the car behind him. They'd asked to drive him, but Dash said no. He hated needing them, but his company's largest customer had included that requirement in their latest contract.

As he made his way to the front porch, the door opened.

Wes motioned him inside and then closed the door. "Have you slept at all?"

"A couple hours." Dash hadn't been watching the clock, but he had woken up, so he'd fallen asleep at some point.

"You look like you pulled three all-nighters." Wes didn't sound impressed.

"Falling asleep wasn't easy. I have a lot on my mind."

"We want to hear all about it. But first, let's get some coffee and food in you."

Dash's stomach clenched. "I'm not—"

"This isn't up for discussion, Wonderkid."

Ugh. He should have known Wes would go all big brother on him. Adam probably would, too. And the others. That wasn't the help Dash needed.

Wes led him to the dining room where Adam, Blaise, Kieran, and Mason sat. A pink box of doughnuts, a platter with bagels, three containers of schmear, sliced fruit, and a dish of scrambled eggs were spread out on the table. A bottle of whiskey from Wes's distillery sat next to a carafe of coffee, a creamer, and a pitcher of orange juice.

"Sit." Wes pulled out a chair for Dash. "If Paige hears you haven't slept or eaten, she'll be on us when she gets here later."

Dr. Paige Regis was not only Wes's fiancée, but she'd also been his oncologist before he went into remission. Ever since the start of the new year, she'd been on them if she thought one wasn't taking care of himself. Dash got hit the hardest because of his eating habits and not making the time to work out regularly. He had a big brother *and* a big sister. Another sign Paige and Wes belonged together.

"I'm not hungry," Dash admitted, even though doughnuts were one of his top ten favorite foods.

Adam prepared a cup of coffee by adding milk and two teaspoons of sugar before sliding it in front of Dash. "Drink this. You look like you're running on fumes."

Flavored water, which was why Dash could use a jolt of caffeine. He hadn't wanted to go into the kitchen this morning. Not if Iris wasn't there.

"Thanks." He took a sip of the hot liquid and

swallowed. "Just the way I like it."

Mason grabbed a bagel. "When was the last time you slept, dude?"

"Please tell me you haven't been living off Mountain Dew and fruit snacks," Adam said.

Those were Dash's go-to junk food. "I slept a little last night, and I haven't eaten those."

Today, at least. Yesterday had been a different story.

Across the table, Kieran studied him. "How are you doing?"

Not trusting his voice, Dash shrugged before drinking his coffee.

Blaise slid a plate toward him. On it was a maple bar with a slice of bacon on top. Dash peeled off the bacon and bit into it.

"You didn't call Henry or Brett?" Adam asked.

"They knew what Iris was planning to do but didn't tell me." It reminded Dash of being the skinny, uncoordinated kid who was all limbs and the last one picked for any team at school. He hated that two people he considered friends had made him feel that way again. "If they'd said something, I could have been prepared with a plan rather than being caught off guard."

Wes covered his bagel in schmear. "Iris might have asked them not to tell you."

"Doesn't matter." Dash didn't care about their reasons. "Friends don't let friends get blindsided."

Kieran stared over the lip of his coffee mug. "So what happened with Iris?"

Dash pushed the plate away. "I went to the cottage last night to talk to her about Henry."

"What would Iris know about him?" Kieran asked.

Dash hesitated. He would have to spill everything. Unfortunately. "I wanted to know if they were dating."

"Henry dating Iris?" Mason laughed, nearly knocking over his glass of orange juice. "Henry doesn't do relationships."

Dash didn't think it was funny, but everyone else did. "He went to see her after the poker game, spent yesterday with her, and kissed her on New Year's Eve. What was I supposed to think?"

"*Are* they dating?" Adam asked.

"No, they're just friends." Saying that brought relief. "Iris told me she'd been out with Henry looking at apartments and that she was resigning. She apologized for giving me less than two weeks' notice."

"Did you have any idea she would quit?" Wes asked.

Dash eyed the doughnut before pushing the plate farther away. "Not a clue."

Blaise leaned forward. "Is Iris looking for another job? Or did she find a new one?"

Dash sighed. "No, to both. She wants to do something new."

"Bummer," Blaise said. "I thought I finally had a chance to hire her as our cook."

Guess the guy had been serious about wanting to offer Iris a job. "She's enrolled at the culinary school. Full-time. She wants to be a chef."

"Iris is talented enough." Kieran grabbed a bagel from the platter. "She should do well."

The others nodded.

Blaise raised his cup of coffee. "She'll be difficult to replace."

Dash swallowed around the lump in his throat. "She's hired people so I won't have to."

"Sounds like Iris." Adam refilled his juice glass. "She goes above and beyond with everything she does for you."

Exactly. Which was why... "You guys need to help me find a way to make her stay."

Silence settled over the dining room. Dash looked at each of the guys, who stared at him funny.

"Double her salary," Mason suggested.

"I told her to name her price. That I'd pay whatever it takes to keep her. She said she didn't need more money." Dash's shoulders sagged. "What am I going to do? I can't lose her."

"She's not yours to lose," Wes said in a matter-of-fact tone.

"Yes, she is." None of them knew how much Iris meant to Dash. "We've been friends forever. And I need her."

"You need her to clean your house, cook, and take care of things for you," Kieran clarified. "What's in it for her?"

Huh? Dash had expected none of them to be on Iris's side. They were *his* friends—*his family*. "I take care of her. She gets a salary with benefits, including medical insurance, and a yearly bonus, a car, and the cottage. You guys hire her, too, so she earns extra money. She does well for herself."

Much better than what she earned working at her parents' restaurant.

Mason shrugged. "You think so, but what does Iris think?"

"She told me she enjoys her job," Dash fired back.

"But she wants to be a chef?" Adam asked.

Nodding, Dash toyed with his napkin. "When we were younger, she wanted to be a chef so she could take over her parents' restaurant when they retired. That was part of her dream until her dad sold it."

"Her other dream was culinary school?" Mason asked.

Dash nodded. "Iris dropped out to take care of her mom. Then she didn't have the money to go back, and her dad had left town, so she worked for me. That was six years ago."

Adam set his coffee on the table. "You need to let her go."

The others agreed.

Dash stiffened. "No."

"Yes," Kieran countered.

"You count on her," Wes said. "But she needs to chase her dream."

"If you hold her back, she might come to resent you," Mason added.

Blaise nodded. "She's helped you for six years. It's time for you to support what she wants to do."

Deep down, Dash knew what they said was true, but… "Can't she do both?"

"Maybe," Wes said. "But going to school full-time and working for you would be exhausting. Her strong work ethic would make her do everything even if you told her she didn't have to."

"True." Dash rubbed his forehead. "But the thought of her leaving me—"

"Stop being so selfish," Blaise said harshly. "You dropped out of college despite what your parents wanted you to do. You had little support except for Iris and your investors until you met us. If Iris means as much to you as you're saying, don't think about how this will affect you. Give her the support you wanted when you chased your dream."

Wes pointed to Blaise. "What he said."

"You mentioned Iris was looking for an apartment," Kieran said.

Dash nodded. "The one she had fell through. She wants to be walking distance to the culinary school so she doesn't have to buy a car yet."

"Wait." Blaise's eyes darkened. "When you said she gets a car, does that mean she's using one of yours?"

Dash nodded. "The Range Rover. It's essentially hers."

"It's not hers if your name is on the title," Adam pointed out.

Dash didn't see what the big deal was. "Semantics."

Blaise shook his head. "From your point of view, maybe, but not from hers. Iris has been with you for six years. She has literally nothing. No home of her own. No car of her own. No free time of her own because you expect her to work at parties on her days off."

"She enjoys doing that," Dash countered.

"You're not listening." Blaise's jaw jutted forward. "You might think you've been taking care of her, but all you're doing is controlling her life. Taking care of someone is allowing them to live their life and being there if they need you, not bubble-wrapping them so they never know when they need help."

Mason did a double take. "I'm impressed, Mortenson."

Blaise's cheeks reddened. "Thanks, but it's Hadley's influence."

"No matter. Blaise is correct." Wes focused on Dash. "Give, not provide, Iris a car. She can stay in the cottage and still be around."

Around would be better than gone. Last night, Dash should have given her the car she drove, but then he remembered why she needed an apartment. His throat tightened. "The husband and wife she hired are moving in there."

"Iris hired two people to take her place?" Mason asked him.

"Three." Dash ignored his friends' surprised faces. "She does a lot for me."

"More than one person should," Adam said under his breath.

"Dude." Mason shook his head. "Why don't you buy a condo downtown for her to live in? Tell her it's an investment, and that way she can save her money for when she graduates."

"That's not a bad idea," Adam said to Mason, who beamed from the compliment.

Kieran nodded. "A supportive friend would do that."

"I bet Laurel Matthews would decorate the place for you, too," Blaise added.

Brett's wife was an interior designer who had worked on several of their homes.

"I can do that." Except for the timing. "The only problem is Iris has to move out Thursday."

"Pay cash and demand a quick closing," Adam suggested.

Mason nodded. "She could stay in a hotel or with you if you loan her a car."

Dash ran over the idea in his head. "Buying a place would mean I could make sure she's living somewhere safe. Unless she finds an apartment today, this will work. Thanks, Mase."

Mason fist-bumped him. "You're welcome."

But there was still one problem. Dash leaned back in his chair. "I just hate Iris won't be working for me."

"We can't have everything," Adam joked.

"Though we can have most things," Mason quipped.

Money, however, couldn't buy what Dash wanted most. Still, if Iris lived in a place he owned, that would give them another reason to see each other.

"Now that you have a plan, eat and then you can take a nap in the guest bedroom," Wes ordered. "You shouldn't have driven over here as tired as you are."

The others laughed.

"Lawnmower parent," someone across the table muttered.

"Be careful or we'll start calling you Dad." Fighting a yawn, Dash pulled his plate toward him. He picked up the bar and bit into it. The sugary sweetness and maple icing blended perfectly together. The way he and Iris once did. They would go back to being best friends. He would make sure of it.

And he had a feeling this plan might help get them to where they used to be—inseparable.

Chapter Six

Fighting the urge to shimmy her shoulders, Iris wiggled her toes inside her suede boots. As she stood in the second-floor apartment, anticipation flowed through her.

Talk about perfect.

Smaller—more like a studio with a sleeping alcove—than a one bedroom, but the kitchen had been updated with appliances, cabinets, and countertops. The hardwood floors, crown molding, high ceilings, and picture rail gave the place character. The well-kept building was only two blocks from the culinary institute. So many plusses. The biggest negative was the communal laundry room was in the basement. Although, that would give her extra reading time each week. But…

The couch with throw pillows, the masculine bedding, photographs on the wall, and other items around the place told her someone lived here. The listing hadn't given a move-in date but said "ready soon." That could mean anything.

"When will the apartment be available?" she asked.

The manager, a woman named Candace with frosted hair and a wide smile, checked the paperwork she had with her. "On February first. Not quite three weeks."

Three days would have been better, but Iris would take weeks over a month or longer. That would cost more than she'd wanted and make her budget tighter, but she preferred this apartment to the one she'd lost to water damage and the others she'd seen yesterday. All she had to do was find a temporary place nearby or close to public transportation. Not ideal, but doable.

She glanced around again, imagining where she would put furniture. Why was she hesitating? This was exactly what she wanted. "I'll take it."

The woman's smile spread, deepening her laugh lines. "I knew this unit would go fast. You're the first to see it."

"A friend told me about the listing. It must have been right after it went live when I emailed you."

Iris hadn't been able to sleep after talking to Dash, so she'd heard the notification from Henry's text and clicked on the link he sent. She hadn't wanted to wait for him to wake up to look at the place so she took the earliest appointment offered.

"What do you need from me?" she asked.

"Here's the application. The fee is forty dollars paid by check." The manager gave Iris a form and a pen. "If you complete this now, I'll run a credit report and let you know on Monday."

Tomorrow. That wouldn't be a long wait.

Iris stood at the kitchen counter, filled out her information, and wrote a check. She rarely carried her checkbook but had learned many places wouldn't accept cash for the application fee. As soon as she handed over everything, she surveyed the apartment once more, imagining what she needed to buy to fill the place.

Excitement welled inside her. Iris wanted to tell Dash. Though he might not care. Henry would. He seemed as excited about the changes she was making as Iris was.

The manager scanned the application. "Looks complete. I'll see you out."

"Thank you." Iris glanced over her shoulder. She couldn't wait to make this place homey, but she wouldn't need too many things to start. A bed, a dresser, a kitchen table, and chairs were top on the list. The mattress she would buy new. She would scour the internet and thrift stores for the rest while she had access to a car.

As she followed the woman to the lobby and said goodbye, a text notification buzzed on Iris's cell phone. Once outside the building, she removed her phone from her purse.

Dash: *Watching football at Wes's place. Will be home later. If you don't have plans for dinner, come by the house and join me. Ordering Thai.*

Iris read the message twice. Happiness flowed through her. This time, nothing would hold her back. She didn't care about the people passing by on the sidewalk or the cars on the street. She shimmied her shoulders. "Yes!"

After Dash's reaction last night, she'd thought he was upset at her. He hadn't said he understood, but maybe he'd had time to sleep on it. Whatever was going on in that brain of his, inviting her to dinner was a good sign. They hadn't done that in far too long. Thai food had been second to pizza when they'd lived in his apartment and after they moved into the house. She typed a reply.

Iris: *Sounds great. Be sure to get spring rolls and extra peanut sauce.*
Dash: *Always, even though I'll leave those to you.*
Iris: *What time?*
Dash: *Around seven.*
Iris: *I'll be there.*

THE DEAL BREAKER

She would bake brownies for dessert. Dash loved those as much as cookies. Who was she kidding? He enjoyed whatever she baked. The apartment wasn't hers yet, and she didn't want to jinx anything, but she had a good feeling about it. Maybe losing the first place had happened for a reason.

That reminded her. She needed to send another text.

Iris: *Thanks for your help yesterday and for the link last night. The place is beyond perfect! I'm the first to apply. I hope I get it. Find out tomorrow.*
Henry: *Let me know as soon as you hear.*
Iris: *I will.*
Henry: *Have you told Dash?*
Iris: *We talked last night. He wasn't happy, but he invited me to dinner tonight.*
Henry: *Going out?*
Iris: *His house. Takeout.*
Henry: *Have fun. And don't do anything I wouldn't do.*
Iris: *Well, I'm not one to gorge on Thai food. Now the brownies I'm bringing…*
Henry: *Enjoy!*

Iris would.

That evening, she carried the plate of brownies into the main house, closing the French door with her hip. Music played. A light floral scent lingered on the air.

A glance at the table made her stumble.

Iris fell forward. Her left arm shot out to balance herself while she clutched the plate with her right hand. Somehow, she righted herself and didn't hit the floor. Dessert survived, too.

Her pulse raced as if she and the brownies had gone splat on the floor. She took a breath and another.

Except...

She studied the table, unease growing with each passing second.

Seeing the tablecloth, coordinating napkins, plates, glasses, silverware, and a vase full of flowers was unexpected. Someone had gone to a lot of trouble. Dash knew where things were kept, but that was about it. Which meant Raina probably set the table.

Iris's heart fell.

Who was she kidding? It plummeted to her feet and kept right on going to the earth's core.

Raina must have returned from her weekend away and decided to have a romantic dinner with Dash, not knowing he'd invited Iris over.

No biggie. She didn't want to be a third wheel.

I'll leave the brownies where Dash can see them.

But as she set the plate on the table, disappointment weighed heavy on her.

Shake it off.

She would, but first, she wanted to get out of here

fast. Dash had never been big on PDA with the women he dated, but Raina was always touching or kissing him.

Iris headed to the door.

"Hey. Where are you going?" Dash asked. "The food will be here in a few minutes."

She grabbed the door handle. "I don't want to be in the way."

"How would you be in the way?" He sounded confused.

Walking out without answering would be rude. She let go and faced him.

Dash's hair was messy as if he'd been dragging his hands through it. He wore sweatpants and a T-shirt with a vintage game controller graphic on the front. Not exactly date night attire, but Dash dressed like that on weekends.

She motioned to the table. "You're having dinner with Raina."

A puzzled expression formed on his face. "I'm eating with you."

"But the table…"

As his chest puffed out, a satisfied smile spread. "Not bad, huh?"

She stared in disbelief. "You did this?"

He nodded. "I can't take full credit. I watched a video. Looks good, right?"

"Y-yes." He must have left Wes's house early to have time to do this. Iris couldn't believe he'd gone to this much trouble. Not for her. And the way he wasn't one hundred percent sure of his efforts was cute. "I figured Raina had done it."

"Nope." He stood taller. "Be careful, or it might go to my head."

That made Iris smile. She glanced at the two place settings. "It's just us tonight?"

"You and me, so get over here." Dash pulled out a chair "And sit."

She did. This was…weird. In the past, they'd eaten in front of the television, never at the table. And what was up with the flowers? "You've gone to a lot of trouble for takeout."

"You deserve it for all you've done for me."

The doorbell rang.

As she went to stand, he touched her shoulder. "I'll get it."

He headed to the front door.

What was going on? Dash wasn't acting like himself. The forks and knives were in the correct positions. Usually, he resorted to paper towels because those were easier than finding the cloth napkins.

A minute later, he returned. "Dinner is served."

Dash placed each of the containers on the table, and she opened them. He grabbed two bottles of beer from the fridge, removed the caps, and set one in front of her.

"A toast." As soon as he sat, he raised his bottle.

THE DEAL BREAKER

"To new beginnings and old friends. Forever friends."

Even though this Dash was nothing like the friend Iris had grown up with, she tapped her beer against his and drank.

He offered her a spring roll. "How did the apartment hunting go today?"

"I filled out an application for one. I'll find out if I get the place tomorrow." Warmth rushed through her. "It's small, but has everything I wanted."

Dash's smile faltered for an instant before it returned. "I hope you get it."

"Thank you." She appreciated his sincere tone. "I'm crossing every appendage."

"I'll do the same." Dash spooned white rice onto his plate and then passed her the container. "If it falls through, let me know. My portfolio could use an investment property in downtown that had a guaranteed renter."

Her lips formed a perfect o. She couldn't believe he would do that for her. Not after the way he acted last night. Needing a minute, she added rice to her plate. "That's sweet of you to offer, but why?"

His gaze went from the yellow curry to Iris. "What do you mean?"

"Last night, you weren't happy I was leaving."

"I'm sorry." He bit his lip. "You caught me off guard, and I overreacted."

"It's okay, but this is a big change."

"It is." A sheepish expression formed. "I screwed

up. I was being selfish when you told me you were quitting, only thinking of myself. Things haven't been the same between us for a while now, and that's my fault, but I want you to know I support you."

She appreciated his being so forthcoming. On New Year's Day, he'd muttered an "I'm sorry" before handing her a check. He never explained why he hadn't called or left a gift. Which was typical Dash—avoid confrontation at all costs. But that was then. No need to dwell in the past.

"Apology accepted. I'll take all the support I can get." Dash wasn't the most self-actualized person around. He could be rather clueless at times. That told Iris he likely had help seeing the situation more clearly. "You talked to the guys, didn't you?"

He nodded. "They set me straight this morning, but Henry and Brett weren't there. I…didn't invite them."

Of course Dash didn't. She should have realized that might happen. "I asked them not to say anything until I had a chance to talk to you myself, so they were honoring that request. They didn't go behind your back to help me."

"It feels like they did."

Dashiell Cabot might be one of the smartest and wealthiest men in the world, but the geeky teenager whose wavering self-confidence took a big hit with his parents' divorce still called the shots sometimes.

She reached out and covered his warm hand with

hers. "Henry and Brett helped me because you're their friend. It had nothing to do with me."

Dash straightened. "Really?"

"Yes, really. They knew you'd want to make sure I was okay."

"Will you be okay?"

She patted his hand before pulling away. "I will."

He stared at his half-full plate. "Good."

She'd call that a win given his response last night. It was her turn to dish out the delicious-smelling yellow curry. "Guess I owe your friends some pulled pork sliders for all their help."

The corners of his mouth curved upward. "And those bacon-wrapped figs?"

"I'll see what I can do."

"Do you think you'll get the apartment?"

"I'm hopeful I will." She spooned Pad Thai on her plate. "If I get it, I'll need to find a place to live until I can move in on the first."

"Stay here with me." He spoke as if it were one long word, not four of them.

"What?" she asked, wanting to make sure she heard him correctly.

He took a breath. "Stay here. I have plenty of guest bedrooms."

"I know. I'm the one who cleans them." She laughed, more of a nervous giggle since his invitation was unexpected. Maybe even to him.

His cheeks reddened. "You can use the Range

Rover to get back and forth. If you want it permanently—"

"That's too generous, but thanks for the offer." She didn't want him to give her a car. He didn't owe her anything. Taking the bonus—something she'd earned—had been difficult enough. "If I can't find a temporary place—"

"Stop looking." His voice was firmer this time. "Move in and use the car until your apartment is ready."

Iris forced herself to breathe. This would help her out financially and logistically. "You're serious?"

"One hundred percent. Pick a bedroom." He winked. "Well, any that is unused."

The sole occupied one was Dash's. She only went in there to clean or put away his laundry and dry cleaning and set out his clothing. "That would be great, but I don't want to be in the way."

"You won't be," he countered. "We were roommates in a much smaller place."

"True." The apartment was smaller than Dash's garage. But memories of that time brought a smile to her face. "It wasn't much more than a nondescript rectangle with doors and windows, but I loved that place."

"Me, too. Close to our first office, and you made it feel like home. The way you have here." He reached for a food container. "We got along there, so sharing this house will be a cinch."

"I'll be at school for eight hours a day, five days a week." That would be different from when they'd lived together before. She'd been at the apartment most of the time, unless she went with Dash to help at his office. Given his work schedule and her classes, chances were they wouldn't see each other more than they did now.

A heaviness pressed against the center of her chest. She ignored the twinge of disappointment. Their friendship would never be as strong as when they were younger, but she wanted him to be in her life...somehow. If not *friends forever* then *friends for now*. Maybe moving in for a couple weeks would help. "Staying here would make things easier for me, if you're sure I won't be a burden."

Dash's grin lit up his face. "It's settled, then."

"Not so fast." Iris didn't want his generosity to lead to problems for him, and she could think of a big one. "What about Raina?"

He scooped the Pad Thai onto his plate before putting the shrimp pieces back into the container. "What about her?"

"She might not like me staying with you."

Raina was polite to Iris but not overtly friendly. Not surprising since she focused her attention on Dash whenever the two were together. To be honest, Raina had said little to Iris and ignored her most of the time.

Shaking his head, he grabbed two skewers of

chicken satay and then a fried wonton. "Why would Raina care?"

"Because she's your girlfriend."

"You're my friend. You live here already."

For someone so smart, he could be dense at times. "In the cottage, not in the same house."

He pushed the containers toward Iris. "It's not a big deal."

"To you." Even though Dash didn't need her the way he once had, the urge to take care of him was strong. "I'd feel better if you talked to Raina about my staying here before we make this a done deal."

Dash's gaze met Iris's. A beat passed. "If that's what you want, I'll ask her tomorrow, so don't waste time looking for another place."

"Thank you."

"Not a problem." He raised a wonton off his plate. "And it won't be with Raina, either. Trust me."

Iris wanted to, but his girlfriend was a wildcard.

He made a face, one that said *come on*. "When have I ever let you down?"

"Well…" Should she start with the most recent time or—

"Don't answer," he said sharply. "Eat while the food's still hot."

Iris took a bite of the Pad Thai, her favorite. That didn't stop her from feeling all tingly. Not because of the food, but Dash.

He was acting more like his old self. The one

who'd thrown her a surprise birthday party when she turned twenty-one. The one who'd driven to the restaurant to pick her up six years ago when she had nowhere to go. The one who'd had his brand-new house's kitchen remodeled so she could have her dream oven and cooktop. The one who'd binge watched movie series with her before it was the thing to do.

Maybe spending more time together—albeit a meal or bumping into each other in the house—would bridge the disconnect she'd felt with him for so long.

Dash set his fork on his plate and picked up his beer. "Want to watch a movie after dinner?"

Her heart swelled. "I'd love to."

"We can eat the brownies then. It'll be like old times."

Old times? Or new ones?

Nodding, Iris ate a forkful of curry. She couldn't wait to find out because tonight had given her hope that maybe her friendship with Dash wasn't over. Maybe it had just changed a little.

Chapter Seven

Monday evening, Dash rode the elevator to Raina's loft in the Pearl District. His day had started off with a call from his mom, who wanted to use the beach house next week, and asked him to talk to his dad who had the dates blocked off. Dash hadn't had time to get caught up in another squabble. He told her to phone him herself which led to his father's angry voice mail about being bothered by "that woman" and a frustrated message from his mother about "that man."

Dash didn't return either call because he'd been in meetings all afternoon. He'd also received a text from Iris telling him she'd gotten the apartment. The happy face emojis showed him how excited she was about the news. He used other emojis to congratulate her.

He might be torn over her leaving, but he would do his best to be supportive.

At least tonight's dinner with two of his VPs and a potential customer had gone well. They'd sealed a multimillion dollar, five-year contract at the swanky restaurant on the thirtieth floor of a Portland building with a great view of the metro area.

But today had drained him. His parents kept blowing up his cell phone, but he would ignore them as long as he could. Maybe he should sell the beach house, so they had one less thing to fight about. It wasn't as if he'd used it in the last two years.

Dash yawned. All he wanted to do was go home—and he'd thought of doing just that—but he needed to do this to firm up the plans with Iris.

The elevator dinged, and the doors opened. He forced his feet to move.

He stepped out into a lobby area decorated in a style he jokingly referred to as high-end urban hipster. Call him old-fashioned, but he preferred his house with a big yard—what others called an estate—but Raina loved the location and architecture of this building.

Get in. Get out.

That was his plan for tonight.

Dash strode to her unit and knocked.

After opening the door, Raina greeted him with a wide smile.

"Hey." She wore jeans and a turtleneck. Her dark

brown hair fell past her shoulders. Only a little makeup was on her face, which he liked, but her lips glimmered, more sparkly than normal. She must have gone shopping this weekend. "This is a nice surprise."

Dash hugged her and then kissed her cheek. "You look way more relaxed than last week."

"I am. I was in a better mood at work, too." Raina stepped back from him. "Come in."

He entered the apartment. The minimalistic décor—something he'd learned about from Laurel Matthews—featured white and black with gray and yellow accents. The couch was more magazine-worthy than it was comfortable, but that didn't stop him from sitting.

"I wasn't sure I'd see you this week, so I was happy to get your text." Raina sat next to him, leaving no space between them. "Miss me?"

Dash hadn't. Iris had been on his mind this weekend, but he knew better than to admit that. Truth was, he rarely missed anyone, which was why he never understood why any of the guys, except Henry, went crazy when their wives or fiancées weren't around.

He stretched his legs out in front of him. "You needed the time away."

"I did." She scooted closer, nearly parking herself on his lap. "So what's up?"

"Iris quit." The words tasted bitter, but he didn't react to that. "She's moving out of the cottage this week."

Raina's mouth dropped open. "I… That's unexpected."

Dash nodded. "Took me by surprise."

"Does it have anything to do with Henry?"

Even though Iris had said the two were just friends, Dash's muscles bunched. "No."

"Wow." Raina tilted her chin. "I never thought Iris would willingly leave her position with you. It's great she has."

An alarm sounded in his head. "What do you mean by that?"

"Iris does an excellent job, but she's so…attached to you."

He didn't know what Raina was talking about. "We've been friends for over fifteen years."

"Yes, but this will be good for everyone. Especially you." Raina beamed as if he'd handed her a winning lottery ticket. "I'm happy to help pick up some slack."

Huh? What Raina said made no sense. She worked as many hours at her job as Dash did. Sometimes more to prepare for a launch. Besides, he couldn't picture Raina doing his laundry, laying out his clothes for the week, running his errands, or touching his gaming equipment. "Iris hired a husband-and-wife team to handle the house and managing the other staff and a chef."

"That's overkill when you have me."

"You don't have time—"

"I'll make the time." Raina cut him off. "You mean a lot to me. And I know how much you depend on Iris. I want to do that for you."

Too bad the only person he wanted doing anything for him was Iris. "Thanks, but the people who've been hired can handle it."

"Maybe, but this is the perfect time for us to reexamine our relationship." She placed her hand on his chest. Her fingernails were painted black. They hadn't been last week. A manicure must have been part of her spa day treatment.

And the fact he was focusing on her hand instead of this conversation told him all he needed to know. "That's not why I came over."

Raina shrugged, but she showed no indifference. Only interest and anticipation shone in her eyes. "Don't you think it's time we got more serious about each other?"

No. Dash wanted to say that but pressed his lips together instead. He didn't want to get into an argument. "We haven't been dating that long."

He couldn't remember the actual date when they'd first gone out. Late September or early October? Whatever it was, only a few months had passed.

"Longer than your friends who are engaged or married," Raina countered. "Didn't you tell the guys, 'When you know, you know'?"

"Yes." Except Dash didn't know how he felt

about Raina.

Not really.

He enjoyed spending time with her. She put up with his work schedule and gaming. They had fun and shared many common interests. He appreciated that she was low maintenance and how she got along with his friends and their significant others. Beyond that…

Dash didn't love her. He wasn't even sure if he could ever love anyone.

"They must have known they'd found 'the one,'" she said.

As a three-carat-diamond sized lump lodged in his throat, he nodded. Henry had brought Brett and Laurel together through one of his birthday adventures, but the two were meant to be a couple. It had just taken them time to figure that out. Adam and Cambria had been the first to fall in love and marry. Kieran and Selah followed. Mason and Rachael had been next. Blaise had hired Hadley to win the bet, but he ended up marrying the matchmaker instead. And then there was Wes and Paige, two people who were a perfect match. Yes, his friends had each found their one, but that wasn't a topic for discussion.

Not now.

Or ever.

Dash swallowed. It didn't help. He cleared his throat. Time for a subject change. "I came over tonight because I want to tell you something."

Her eyes twinkled, as if a million stars had turned

on just for him. She leaned toward him. "I'm listening."

He wiped his hands again. "Iris needs a place to live for a couple of weeks until she can move into her apartment. I told her she could stay with me."

Raina stiffened. "At your house?"

Dash nodded, not liking the way her smile had vanished. Tension emanated from her, too.

"Why would you do that?" Her words came out clipped and rushed.

"She needs a place to stay."

"A hotel would be better. It's the best solution."

Okay, he hadn't expected that. But Iris had warned him. "Why?"

"Because you're my boyfriend, and she…" Raina looked away.

"What?"

"Iris will use this to her advantage."

Dash scratched his chin. "I'm not following along with this."

"She's crazy about you and will try to make you fall in love with her."

He stared dumbfounded. "You realize Iris has had fifteen years to do that, and she hasn't."

"I see how she looks at you."

"I'm never home, or if I am, she's not there." Dash couldn't believe Raina was saying this about Iris. "You said it yourself. I'm more her boss than her best friend."

Raina raised her chin. "Then Iris wants to seduce her boss."

The words hung in the air as if surrounded by a dialogue bubble.

"That's—"

"The truth," Raina finished for him.

"Iris has never said or implied anything like that." Dash thought back to when they'd been younger. There'd been that one time they almost kissed, but Iris had appeared as embarrassed as he was. They'd made their deal to be friends forever and never mentioned it again. She would have never agreed if she wanted more. "Not ever."

"You might not have noticed, but I have."

Except he hadn't. "This is nonsense."

"No, it's not." Raina touched his arm. "That's why you need to tell her you changed your mind about her moving in."

"I offered. I can't take it back."

"Then find her another place to stay. Somewhere cheap."

His muscles tightened. "Cheap?"

"Iris is the help, babe. Not one of us. Don't go overboard and put her up at a five-star hotel."

"That's…" Dash couldn't get the words out. He felt as if he were seeing Raina for the first time. No, that wasn't correct. He'd thought she had acted differently when she called on Saturday night. He didn't like having to defend his friend, but he would.

"Iris is returning to culinary school to become a chef."

"That doesn't change who she really is. A housekeeper."

His temper spiraled, but he forced himself to remain under control. "Iris is so much more than that. I wouldn't be where I am without her. She's been an important part of my life for the past fifteen years."

"That's why I'm not comfortable having her stay with you."

"It won't even be three weeks."

"Three days would be too long."

What she was implying, not only about Iris but him, slammed into Dash like a runaway freight train. A bitter taste coated his throat. "Do you think I'd cheat?"

"She's pretty and wants you. A person could be tempted."

His mouth watered. He thought he might be sick. His parents' cheating had nearly destroyed him. To be accused of doing the same thing… "I would never do that."

"But Iris would."

"You don't know her." He scrubbed his face with his hand. "She wouldn't."

"That's easy to say. Oh, wait. I think I may have the perfect solution to this." Raina perked up. "If I move in with you…"

"I'm not ready for that."

"Then Iris can't stay with you." Raina's voice rose an octave.

Oh, man. Dash dragged his fingers through his hair. He hadn't expected this reaction, but Iris had. Somehow, she'd known. Henry had also said Raina wasn't the one for him. What had they noticed that Dash hadn't? "I didn't think this would be a big deal."

"It is. And I won't apologize for feeling this way." Raina angled her shoulders toward him. "We have something good here. Something that could last. I want nothing to ruin it. Having Iris stay with you will."

That sounded a lot like an ultimatum. "Are you asking me to choose between you and her?"

"I'm asking you not to allow Iris to come between us and the wonderful future we could have together."

Yep, an ultimatum.

Dash's blood boiled.

This was ridiculous. And it was ending now.

He wanted distance, but he was trapped between the sofa's armrest and Raina. "I told you I wasn't interested in a serious relationship."

"That was months ago. Things have changed between us." As she ran her finger along his jawline, he turned away from her touch. But that only made her rub his shoulder. "You spent Christmas with my family."

"Because you invited me." And he was too much of a wimp to say no.

Ugh. This was all his fault. He glanced at the ceiling.

There was only one thing he could do—something he'd never done before. "I've enjoyed spending time with you."

She smiled. "Same."

"We've had fun together, but I'm not ready for more." Dash didn't want to hurt her, but he was done. The way she talked about Iris was a huge turnoff and red flag. He'd mentioned his parents' cheating and divorce, so Raina knew how he felt about that. "I'm sorry if I misled you, but my feelings haven't changed since we first went out."

Raina's jaw tensed before she forced a smile. "I'm willing to wait."

"This isn't working. We each want different things. Plus, anyone who is part of my life needs to respect Iris, not believe she and I would cheat behind their back."

"I can try." Raina's eyes gleamed. "I mean, I will. Do."

It was too late. She was only saying what she thought he wanted to hear.

"Take care of yourself." He stood, not feeling an ounce of regret or sadness, only relief. "I'll see myself out."

* * *

Before his drive home, Dash sent a text asking Iris to meet him in the kitchen in thirty minutes. He stopped at an ice cream shop on NW 23rd Avenue for a pint of Honey Lavender and one of Sea Salt with Caramel Ribbons. When he walked in the house, he found her in the pantry. Not where he expected her to be at this hour.

He set the bag on the island. "What are you doing?"

"Making a note of what was out of place. I'll speak with Tony and Janice tomorrow about where things go." Iris held a pen and notepad with scribbles on it. She noticed what was on the island, and a smile erupted, lighting up her face. "You bought ice cream."

Seeing her so happy pleased him, erasing the time he'd been at Raina's. "We need to celebrate your new apartment."

She bounced on her tiptoes. "You're the best."

Her compliment shouldn't make him feel so good, but it did. Dash removed the two pints. "Your favorite flavor and mine."

"Oh, thank you." After setting her pen and paper on the counter, she removed two bowls from a cabinet before pulling out the scooper and two spoons from nearby drawers. "Thank goodness I hadn't eaten a brownie already or I wouldn't be able to button my jeans."

He glanced at her in a pair of black leggings and a pink T-shirt that fell past her hips. "Isn't that what leggings and yoga pants are for?"

She stuck out her tongue at him.

Dash laughed. "You know I'm joking. You could eat the whole pan, and it wouldn't affect you."

"Now you're really joking." She patted her left hip. "If I did that, it would go right here."

"Nothing wrong with that."

"There isn't," she agreed. "I enjoy food too much to be as thin as Raina. Tonight I plan on eating an extra scoop of ice cream."

"It's all yours."

Iris scooped the first flavor into a bowl, stuck a spoon in the ice cream, and slid the dish his way. "Here's yours."

She fixed hers. "And this one is mine."

"You sound like you can't wait for a taste."

"I can't."

One bite had her moaning with delight and making him happy she was enjoying it so much. He would have to bring home dessert more often.

She waved her spoon at him. "You know the way to my heart."

"Ice cream or chocolate bars with nuts." He didn't hesitate answering, even if it had been years since he'd brought her either. "Though chocolate-covered strawberries work in a pinch."

Nodding, she ate another spoonful. "This is the perfect way to celebrate my new place."

That reminded him. "Whenever you're ready, you

can start moving in."

Her gaze jerked to his. "It's okay with Raina?"

The hope in her eyes touched Dash unexpectedly, sparking something inside him. Trying to figure out what he was feeling, he ate a spoonful of ice cream.

"Did she say it was okay for me to stay here?" Iris asked again before he could answer.

Dash looked at his spoon for a moment before staring at her. "We broke up."

"Tonight?"

He nodded.

Iris's nose scrunched. "But I thought everything was going well. What happened?"

He didn't know how to answer. "It was time."

She stared at him. "You don't look upset about it."

"I'm not." He took another bite of ice cream. That told him he'd done the right thing tonight. "It was the same old story. Just a different name and face."

"She wanted to get more serious?"

"She mentioned moving in with me." He wouldn't tell Iris how she'd come up in the discussion or she would blame herself. "And the future came up. But I'm not ready for any of that."

"So she broke up with you."

It wasn't a question because that was what always happened. "Actually, I broke up with her."

Iris lowered her spoon. "You've never done that."

"It was time I did." His wanting to keep the peace had only caused him problems. "We saw things differently. I didn't want to lead her on. I would only end up hurting her more if we stayed together."

His relief at no longer dating Raina had only increased since he arrived home.

She studied him as if he were one of the special recipe cards from her late mother. "I'm sure that was difficult for you."

"It needed to be done." He didn't want Raina anywhere near Iris or him. "I should probably let Hadley know."

Iris stared at her bowl. "She can fix you up with someone else."

"I'm not interested in using Hadley's services," Dash admitted. "I only went out with Raina that first time to help Blaise. I never thought I'd end up dating her regularly, but I don't plan on being set up again."

Spending Christmas away had set all this in motion, but he didn't blame Raina for that. He'd been the one to blow up his friendship with Iris. Now, he needed to make amends—show her how much she meant to him. He had less than three weeks until she moved into her new apartment. Dash would do whatever it took to make the most of each day.

Chapter Eight

Even though Iris preferred romantic comedies, she enjoyed sitting on the couch and watching the action-adventure movie with Dash. The film had a decent plot and romantic storyline to keep her interest amid the gunfire and explosions. The brownies didn't hurt.

The plate sat on the cushion between them. She took another one—her third, not that anyone was keeping track. This was a celebration, so calories didn't count. At least, that was what she would go with if Dash asked. Not that he cared about anything but the film.

A side-eye glance showed him engrossed with what played on the television screen. Raina hadn't come up again during dinner. The breakup appeared to be a thing of the past. Iris wasn't that surprised since he'd never shown emotion when a relationship ended. He usually claimed it was inevitable and never mentioned the woman again.

Dash paused the movie before looking her way. "You're watching me more than the TV."

Iris's cheeks burned. "Just making sure you're okay."

"About?"

Was he serious? Then she remembered this was Dash. "The breakup."

"I'm fine," he blurted. "It was bound to happen, eventually."

Inevitable. She was correct. Raina had been the same as the other women he dated. Relief surged through Iris. Strange, because she wanted him to be happy.

"Someday it won't feel that way." He deserved somebody to love, even if hearts, flowers, and violins weren't his thing. "You just haven't met the right woman."

He grinned. "Not sure she's out there since Wes told me video game characters didn't count."

Iris laughed. "Well, if one came to life, she would be all over you."

His brows lifted. "You think?"

"You're a catch."

It was his turn to laugh. "We both know my net worth is the biggest appeal. I'm too nerdy for most women."

"You're you. Authentic. Real. That's all that matters. Who cares if you're eccentric?"

"Eccentric is another word for weird." He shifted on his end of the couch so he faced her. "I am that."

"A good weird," she added, knowing his joking was a self-defense mechanism. "Somewhere, there's a woman who will feel as if she's won the lottery when you fall in love with her and she with you."

"If," Dash corrected. "Not when. I'm not sure love even exists."

"It does, which is why I said *when* not *if*." Someday he would believe love conquered all. "You deserve a happily ever after."

He got a faraway look in his eyes. "Do you still want one?"

Her lips parted. "You remembered?"

Dash shrugged, but his gaze never wavered from hers. "I may not be good at dates and other stuff."

That was why she filled in his calendar each month and ordered or made reservations for the occasion. Janice would take over doing that tomorrow. "That's what digital calendars are for."

He nodded. "You couldn't stop talking about having a June wedding, a husband, four point five children, a dog, and a cat."

"Three kids and you forgot the house with a fireplace and big yard."

His lopsided grin made him seem ten years younger. A part of her wished they could go back to when they were besties. The two of them against the world.

"I was close," he said. "Cut me some slack."

"You were. And I will," she agreed. "I'm impressed. I told you that before my mom got sick…"

Dash pushed the plate toward her. "Have another."

"Enabler."

"I believe that would be you for baking them."

Iris did the only thing she could. She took a brownie and bit into it.

He watched her with an odd expression, one she hadn't seen before.

Iris wiped her mouth with the back of her hand. "Do I have something on my face?"

"No." He smiled. "You seem…happier."

"I am." Though she hadn't expected him to notice. The fact he had was nice. "I have a place to live temporarily before I move into my apartment. I'm returning to culinary school. And we're hanging out and eating brownies."

"I'm happy, too. I want…" He stared at the plate on the cushion.

Uh-oh. Was his social awkwardness coming out? She moved toward him. "What?"

He rubbed his lips together. "I want us to be best friends again."

It was as if he'd been reading her mind. Her heart

overflowed with joy. "I'd like that, too."

Relief shone in his eyes. "Great."

She nodded. "Maybe we should try being better friends first."

"Friends," he repeated in an odd voice.

"Besties can grow from that." And keep her from being disappointed if it didn't work out. Dash might have the best intentions, but they weren't teenagers with tons of free time. He had so many other responsibilities, and she didn't want to get hurt again.

"Deal." He hit play on the remote. "We should finish watching this, or we'll be up too late."

As the movie played, Iris finished her brownie. Dash stretched his arm across the top of the sofa. His hand was warm against her neck. Then, unexpectedly, his fingers played with her hair.

She froze, unsure what was happening.

Dash had hugged her and wiped her tears over the years. Okay, he'd touched her shoulder, arm, and hand.

But he'd never done this. Not once when they'd watched a movie in the past.

She gulped.

It had been a couple years since they'd watched something together. Maybe he didn't notice. Maybe he normally did this with his dates. Maybe touching a woman's hair was what he enjoyed doing while watching a movie.

Iris didn't dare move or talk, afraid anything she

did would ruin their rekindled friendship.

Emphasis on friendship.

She tried to relax, but tension built in her shoulders.

Dash's attention was on the screen. He didn't appear to have a clue what he was doing. Which meant maybe he didn't realize he was touching *her*.

A part of her almost wished he had.

Wait. What?

She swallowed.

This was Dash.

Her friend.

Her soon-to-be best friend again if things worked out. And she wanted it to. More than she thought possible. That meant…

Daydreaming or fantasizing anything else was going on was wrong.

Wrong. Wrong. Wrong.

Just friends was enough. It had to be.

* * *

Monday morning arrived much too soon for Iris. A sleepless night over-analyzing Dash had left her exhausted. She wanted to hit the snooze button but didn't because she had work to do.

Getting dressed, she yawned.

A nap wouldn't happen with the training and packing to do today, but she would go to bed early.

The last thing she needed was to catch a cold before classes started. She slid her feet into her suede boots, shrugged on her jacket, and headed outside into darkness.

Unlike her, the sun was still asleep. It wouldn't peek above the horizon for another hour. A light drizzle fell, but the path, illuminated by lights, wasn't too wet. The cool temperature, however, seeped into her. She shivered.

Iris quickened her steps. As soon as she was inside, the heat enveloped her like a long-lost friend, making her feel warm and cozy as she had last night. She pulled off her jacket and removed her boots, leaving everything in the mudroom.

She yawned again.

In the kitchen, she made a pot of coffee with the ridiculously expensive beans Dash loved. He took an insulated cup with him to work each morning, but today, she needed the caffeine to keep her going. As the coffee brewed, filling the air with a fragrant scent, she placed two frosted Pop-Tarts on a plate. Not the expected breakfast of a twenty-eight-year-old billionaire, but he enjoyed them, so she kept a few boxes in the pantry, stocking up when they were on sale, so he never ran out.

As she unloaded the dishwasher, she mentally planned out what she needed to do before Janice, Leo, and Tony arrived.

"Good morning." Dash's hair was still damp,

curling at the ends. He wore a pair of khaki pants, a light blue oxford, and brown dress shoes, the Italian ones Henry had suggested Dash buy. The casual style suited him. Instead of sitting at the island's bar, he placed his breakfast in the toaster.

Not his usual MO. "I could have done that."

"You usually do." He sat on a stool. "But I'm not helpless in the kitchen."

Trying not to laugh, she stared down her nose. "Say what?"

"I am one hundred percent trained in using the toaster and microwave thanks to your detailed instructions."

"That was to preserve this gorgeous gourmet kitchen from a fire."

"Come on. It was more smoke than flames."

Iris filled a cup three-quarters of the way full with coffee, added cream, and two teaspoons of sugar. She set the drink in front of him. "You ruined the microwave."

"I know. I know." He sighed. "You don't need to microwave anything that's not frozen for more than five minutes."

"Especially s'mores."

They'd been through this before, but she enjoyed the back-and-forth. Maybe they could still be best friends. Though she didn't know what was up with his twirling her hair.

Maybe coffee would help. She poured herself a cup.

"Admit it." He rested his elbows on the island. "The new microwave was better. More settings and buttons to push."

"It works. That's all that matters to me." She didn't get into the high-tech gadgets and gizmos he bought, but Dash enjoyed having the latest and greatest technology in the house, so she learned to use them. "But Tony's impressed."

"Who's Tony?"

"Your personal chef." She placed the two Pop-Tarts on the plate and set it in front of Dash. "He'll prepare fresh dinners for you during the week, and meals you can heat up on the weekend unless you need him for a dinner or party."

"He's flexible with his days and hours?"

"Very."

Her former culinary school classmate had been so thankful for this job. The restaurant where he worked closed, so he'd needed a new position.

Iris yawned. "You'll like him, and you'll love his cooking."

"Tired?"

She handed him a napkin. "A little. I didn't sleep that great."

Concern clouded his gaze. "Do you feel okay?"

"I'm fine. Just a lot on my mind right now." Not sleeping well was a perfectly normal response when everything in her life was changing, and Iris couldn't stop thinking about Dash. She sipped her coffee.

He wiped his mouth with the napkin. "So I was thinking…"

"Cha-ching," she joked. "That means another billion will soon be added to your net worth."

"Ha-ha, but I was thinking about you."

She flinched. "Me?"

"You took no vacation time over the past six years other than your staycation at Christmas. But I'm not counting that since you planned and catered my New Year's Eve party."

"Doing that is my job."

"And vacation time is a benefit. I'm paying you for the unused time."

Had he offered her vacation time six years ago? Iris didn't remember. Either way… "I could have traveled if I'd wanted to, but I didn't want to go somewhere by myself."

"I should have told you to take the time off, even if you stayed home. That's what we require company employees to do."

Her insides twisted. She didn't like being lumped in with those others. What she did had been as much for Dash as earning a living. "I work for you. It's not—"

"It's happening." He sipped his coffee. "I emailed my accountant to calculate what you're owed."

She had no idea how much vacation pay she received a year, but that would get her closer to her goal of buying a used car. Funny how Dash was funding her return to school and life for the next eighteen or so months. "Thank you."

"No, *thank you*. You've earned it."

Iris lifted one shoulder. "Having extra money in my bank account is never a bad thing."

He smiled. "You sound like Brett when he puts on his Mr. Finance tie."

She laughed because whenever Brett wore a tie, he was totally in business mode. "He may have said that when he was helping with my budget."

"Knew it." Dash bit into one of the frosted Pop-Tarts.

Iris glanced at the time on the microwave. "Hey, you'll be late if you don't take off right now."

"I'm going in later this morning."

"I don't remember seeing a meeting or appointment on your schedule." She checked his calendar before she got out of bed.

"That's why this is the perfect morning to play hooky."

Iris did a double take. "You never played hooky before. Not even when you were in school."

He shrugged. "Guess I'm overdue."

She studied him. Same killer blue eyes and long, thick lashes. His hair fell over his forehead with the same curve. The scar at his left temple after an incident with a snow shovel was still there, too. But…

Iris placed her hands on her hips. "Who are you and what have you done with the real Dash Cabot?"

He laughed. "I promise it's me."

"But you need things to be the same. Like to an OCD level, no offense."

"None taken."

"What's going on?" she asked, curious.

He shrugged.

"Come on," she pressed.

"I'm serious about us being best friends again. That can't happen if we don't spend time together."

His words touched her, but she was having a difficult time wrapping her mind around this. "It's Monday. Your busiest day. Won't you start the week off behind? Something you hate happening."

"I'll delegate because I'd rather make up for lost time with you."

Her heart bumped. Something it hadn't done around Dash in a long time, but it didn't mean anything. They were trying to find their footing again. "That's sweet."

His smile lit up his eyes. "What should we do?"

"Well, Janice, Leo, and Tony will be here in an hour." She tapped her chin. "You could help me decide on which bedroom to stay in."

"The one across from mine is the biggest."

"No, no, no." She shook her head for added emphasis. "I know how loud you listen to music and the TV. You talk to your gaming friends at all hours. Not to mention conference calls with Asia and Europe at strange times."

"Sounds like you've picked one."

She laughed. "Maybe I have. The farthest from yours."

"That's the smallest."

"I won't be there long, and I don't have many things."

He blew out a breath. The corners of his mouth curved downward.

"If that's what you want." He sounded…dejected. "Tell me when you want to move your stuff."

"I will." Iris didn't know what he was thinking, but she missed his smile. Maybe she could bring it back. "So, do we need any roommate rules? Such as swimsuits required in the hot tub."

"Spoilsport." A smile tugged on his lips.

That was better. "Hey, it's been a few years since we lived together."

"You're in my house all the time."

"Not twenty-four seven."

"Fine." He ate another bite. "I have no idea what you do in the cottage when you're alone, but because of you and the maintenance crew, I never walk around the house in my underwear."

An image of him in his boxer briefs formed in her mind. She knew what he wore since she washed and folded his laundry. Her mouth went dry. Heat rushed up her neck. "That's a good rule for both of us. The bedrooms have attached bathrooms, so we won't need to walk around in a towel, either."

"I forgot about towels." He smirked as if wanting to embarrass her more. "But we can't make that a rule."

"Why not?" The question catapulted out because she preferred to see him fully dressed. She didn't usually picture her friends in underwear or a towel and looking so…hot. Even now she was noticing the top buttons undone on his shirt. Her cheeks burned.

"What if the new staff forgets to bring up my clean clothes from the laundry?"

She eyed him warily, unsure if he was teasing. He couldn't be flirting. That was beyond his comfort level…and hers. "You're kidding, right?"

"You don't expect me to dress in dirty clothes, do you?"

Dressing. Undressing. This was not the conversation she expected to have today or any day with him. "You have a closet and dresser full of clothes. I purchased them for you."

"You know me."

At this moment, Iris wasn't sure she did.

Dash flashed the most perfect pair of puppy dog eyes known to man and her heart full-on melted.

What was going on?

"I only like to wear a few things," he continued, oblivious to her pondering whether she'd woken up in an alternate universe. "If those aren't in my room, I'll have to get them myself in nothing but a towel."

"Dude." Her voice came out louder than she

intended. "If you check your clothes before you shower, this is a non-issue. I will also speak to Janice."

"So you're saying the towel thing should be a rule?" The amusement in his voice matched his eyes.

Iris gritted her teeth. "Yes."

"Knock before you enter a room with the door closed?"

She nodded.

"Give advance notice if you're having friends over."

Another nod because she'd never invited anyone to the cottage. Well, other than Henry and Dash. She dated rarely, and most people she knew socially worked in the hospitality industry so mornings and lunch worked better since most worked nights.

"This isn't a rule, but meals are included with your room," he added. "It's easier to cook for two than one."

"That's what I always say, but I lucked out in this case because Tony is an amazing chef." Her taste buds were excited. "You can eat whatever I make on the weekends when he's off."

Dash raised his coffee cup. "This will work out great for me."

"I'm getting the better end of the deal," she admitted.

"You deserve it."

The island separated them, but the way his gaze locked on her, she could almost feel an invisible connection tying them together.

Alternate universe or lack of sleep? At this point, it could be either. She cleared her dry throat. "Thanks."

"It's the least I can do. You never ask me for anything."

"I don't need much." Except for a mom and dad—a family. But Dash could do nothing about that.

His eyes remained on her. "Want is different from need. My parents' divorce sucked, but other than that, I've had it easy. Not you. I'd love to do more to help you, if you'll let me."

"I'm grateful for your support." Not only that, she was relieved to have Dash back in her life. She hoped they could go back to the way things were. She would love that.

A knock sounded, and then the front door opened. "Anyone here?"

"Back here." She grabbed another coffee cup from the cabinet and filled it. "Your new chef is here."

Footsteps sounded on the hardwood floor before Tony appeared in the kitchen. He was six feet tall, built like a running back, and oh-so-easy on the eyes with black hair, brown eyes, and umber skin. Along with his looks, his personality would make him a perfect candidate for a cable TV show.

Tony handed her a small bag. "Try one."

She opened it. "Cookies."

"I tried something new last night." He sounded excited. "I want to know what you think."

Iris removed one. The texture reminded her of shortbread, but the scent was different, spicier. She took a bite. "Delicious. Not what I expected."

"What do you taste?" he asked.

She took another bite and thought for a moment. "Is that anise?"

His smile spread. "That's the secret ingredient."

She ate the rest. "I love the combination of flavors."

Tony winked. "Thought you might."

Dash cleared his throat.

Tony went over to him. "Oh, hey, you must be Dash. Or do you prefer Mr. Cabot?"

"Mr. Cabot is his father," Iris answered, not liking the way Dash glared at his new chef.

Dash pressed his lips together.

She mouthed the words "say something."

His jaw jutted forward. "Using my first name is fine."

That appeared to be the invitation Tony needed. He shook Dash's hand. "Sorry for not noticing you, but when Iris is around, I forget about everything."

She laughed. Tony had hit on all their classmates during their first session. He enjoyed flirting with everyone, including the instructors and custodial crew. It was just his personality, and he was fun to be around, but he wasn't boyfriend material.

"Admit it," she joked. "You say that to everyone."

"I do." Charming dimples formed on either side of Tony's mouth. "But I only mean it with you."

Yeah, right. He reminded her of Henry, except without being a billionaire. Tony was attractive, but he didn't come close to Dash.

She held the bag across the bar. "Want one of Tony's cookies, Dash?"

"No, thanks." His intense gaze sent a burst of lightning through her. "But I wouldn't mind one of yours."

Dash could have whatever he wanted. She gulped. *On second thought...*

Chapter Nine

Dash forced himself not to grimace, but that didn't stop the heat from pooling on his face or sweat beading at his hairline. A drop rolled down his neck slow, as if gravity had no effect and mocked him, followed by another. At this rate, he would need a second shower and to change his shirt before he left for the office.

Tony snickered and gave a thumbs-up sign. "Going to remember that one, boss man."

Just great. Dash had impressed the smooth-talking chef who looked like his parents were a supermodel and an NFL player, but he'd also made a fool out of himself in front of Iris. He should have kept his mouth shut.

Not that he'd tried.

Because Dash had been having fun with her, flirting even. That was unlike him, but he couldn't stop. It was as if on Friday night a switch inside him flipped to the "on" position, making him view Iris differently. That hadn't been a bad thing, given they were acting more like the best friends they used to be. The flirting part, however, was new. So was how much he enjoyed seeing her a bit…flustered. Or rather, he had liked that.

Until Tony arrived.

The guy had some nerve bringing homemade cookies to Iris. Worse, she liked them. Dash had made cookies with her, but he'd eaten the dough instead of helping. He would have to up his game. That would be easy if expensive baubles appealed to her. They didn't. Which meant…

He hadn't a clue what to do.

Oh, Dashiell. You're jealous.

Yeah, he was. The switch had him acting like a jealous teenager. Henry had noticed, mentioning the green-eyed monster. And it was true, especially this morning. Dash wanted to plant himself between Tony and Iris. The chef might as well have "player" tattooed on his forehead. Delicious cookie baker or not, Tony wasn't the type of guy Iris should date.

Wait. Dash's stomach clenched. *Were* they dating?

Iris grabbed something from the counter. A plastic container appeared in front of him. She smiled, almost shyly, but her gaze was full of questions. "No cookies today, but I have the brownies I made yesterday. Will those do?"

He grabbed one, if only to save face. Though eating one was a pleasure, not a sacrifice, even if it was early. "Thanks."

She held out the container to Tony. "Want one?"

Dash pressed his lips together to keep from saying, "Mine."

"Please." The chef took one and bit into it. "Tasty, but I'd try a darker cacao powder next time. That would give the flavor more depth."

Really? The guy might have cooking credentials, but he was an idiot if he didn't love Iris's brownies. He trusted Iris to hire the right people, yet he had serious doubts about this guy. "Your recipe is perfect, Iris. Don't change a thing."

Tony grinned. "Guess I have big shoes to fill if I want to please the man in charge."

Dash had never wanted to say "you're fired" more than he did at that moment. Instead, he ate the brownie. It didn't taste as good as last night. He blamed Tony.

"Did you look over the email I sent you?" Iris asked Tony.

"I did." Tony pulled out a piece of paper from his back pocket and unfolded it. "If I see a brand, only buy that."

She nodded, tilting her head toward Dash. "Or trust me, he'll know and call you out."

Dash's morning with Iris wasn't working out as he'd planned. "I'm not picky."

"You just like what you like," she said without missing a beat.

Tony nodded. "We all have our favorites."

Great. Dash brushed his fingers through his hair. Now they were placating him as if he were a three-year-old.

Iris handed the chef something that resembled a gift card. "Use this for your shopping until your credit card arrives next week. The five hundred dollars should cover the list and leave you extra. If you need additional pans, accessories, or anything else, you might want to wait until you have your card or you can expense them."

"Got it." He tucked the card and the paper back in his pocket. "Nice meeting you, Dash."

With that, Tony headed to the front door.

"He went shopping with me last week." Iris raised her cup. "This time, he's on his own."

A hundred thoughts swirled in Dash's brain. He didn't want to interrogate her, but he wanted answers. He would start with a general statement and go from there. "You've never mentioned Tony before."

Not a question, but that would work.

"After I left the culinary school, we stayed connected via social media." She sipped her coffee. "He was looking for a job with more hours during the day, so he interviewed."

"You held interviews?"

She nodded. "His included cooking your favorite dishes."

Dash scratched his neck. He shouldn't be surprised she was so thorough, but the fact he hadn't known this was happening told him how unaware he'd been about her.

"When did you do this?" he asked.

"Before you came back from your trip to the East Coast. A couple more after the first of the year when you were at work," she explained. "Having people in place and trained will make the transition easier on you."

Something in his chest shifted. The extra effort was for him. "You always take such good care of me."

Iris shrugged. "Someone has to do it."

His parents weren't interested in doing that. He'd gone from being the prize they fought over to being the golden goose who would provide them with whatever they wanted. He only mattered to them when they wanted something. A psychologist could have a field day with his past, but he used his gaming for therapy. He also relied on his friends.

Too bad he hadn't returned the favor for Iris.

But that was what he would do now.

"What's on your list to do this morning?" Dash assumed she had a plan even if she didn't write things down. He wanted to make the most of Tony being at the grocery store.

"Pack the stuff I won't need until I'm in the apartment." Her eyes twinkled. "Want to help me?"

No, because Dash didn't want her to leave, even if she needed to do it for herself. But he couldn't tell her that so he would suck it up.

"Sure." Not that he'd packed when he moved to this house. Iris had overseen the move from the apartment. But he'd done it in college and after he dropped out. Packing was probably like muscle memory. It would all come back to him. Besides, the doing didn't matter. Being with Iris was what mattered. "I'm ready when you are."

* * *

On Wednesday night, Dash sat at his desk, trying not to check the clock. Again.

Outside his window, lights illuminated the parking lot. The building was quiet. A handful of employees were still working, but only the security and janitorial staff were required to be there.

Staying late rarely bothered him. Dash enjoyed working the swing shift. He could accomplish more when people weren't interrupting him and the phone wasn't ringing. But tonight, the only place he wanted to be was home.

With Iris.

To build on their friendship.

That was what he kept telling himself. Except…

Did a friend notice warm eyes and bright smiles and want to touch her all the time? Or how knowing Tony had cooked dinner tonight and she was eating alone, unless the chef had stayed to eat with her, knotted Dash's gut?

Yeah, his blue eyes turned green around the guy.

Childish, yes, especially when Iris didn't sneak peeks at Tony or seem enamored with the chef. But if anyone was spending time with Iris, Dash wanted that person to be him.

He hated that it wasn't tonight.

Spoiled much?

Of course he was.

Being able to afford just about whatever he wanted when he wanted made not getting something harder. Even if it wasn't anything he could buy.

Dash forced his attention on the code. His team had run into a problem, so he'd offered to take a look. That had been three hours ago. Not an easy fix as he'd hoped.

His cell phone buzzed, slicing through the silence in the office.

Ignore it.

What if it's Iris?

Dash glanced at the screen.

Mason: *Are you hosting on Sunday?*

Sunday in January meant football playoff games.

Dash checked his calendar. He'd hosted the New Year's party and poker night. More than his share this month. But if they watched the game at his house, Iris would be there. This would be the perfect time to see how *Tony* handled an event. That way, she could mingle and hang out with Dash. And if Mr. Charming Chef messed up, then he would have a valid reason to fire the guy other than not liking how he flirted with Iris. A win-win.

Dash: *Yes. I'll send out details later.*

First, he needed to make sure Tony could work because he didn't want Iris to do anything more than oversee her new hire. Dash wanted her to be a guest at the party. She'd never been one at any event he'd thrown.

Something Raina had said popped into his mind.

When was the last time you did anything with her outside of the house?

He'd totally forgotten about that.

Idiot.

Him, not her.

Dash owed Raina for telling him that. Now it was up to him to make amends. So far, he'd helped Iris pack her kitchen and bookshelf, eaten dinner with her twice, and watched a movie. He'd enjoyed doing those things with her, but they'd been at his house or her cottage. The football game would be, too. That meant they needed to go out.

He thought for a moment.

Nothing came to mind as to what they should do.

Dash had no idea where Iris liked to go these days. She let him choose the place when they were younger or where they ordered takeout when they were older. Not once had she complained about anything. He'd never noticed that until now.

Self-absorbed much? He needed to watch what he said about Henry. Speaking of the guy, he might know what to do. Dash sent him a text.

Dash: *Where would you take Iris for dinner?*
Henry: *Are we talking me or actually you?*
Dash: *Me, but she would tell me to pick a restaurant. I don't want that.*
Henry: *Well done, Master Dashiell.*
Dash: *So where?*
Henry: *There's a fish place in John's Landing. Super casual, but a favorite of hers.*
Dash: *She's never mentioned it.*
Henry: *You're not a big seafood eater.*
Dash: *I eat salmon.*
Henry: *Which they serve. They also have chicken strips, so you won't starve. Be sure to get the sweet potato fries. She loves those.*
Dash: *Okay.*
Henry: *Raina's been texting the SOs saying you broke up with her.*

Dash: *I did. Is she okay?*
Henry: *Are you having second thoughts about ending things?*
Dash: *No, but I should have listened to you guys and made sure she understood how I felt. I didn't want to hurt her.*
Henry: *You're a good guy, but this is for the best. Trust me.*
Dash: *Okay.*
Henry: *Enjoy a nice meal with Iris and forget everything else.*
Dash: *I will.*
Henry: *But remember to give her flowers.*
Dash: *Really?*
Henry: *I told you to trust me.*
Dash: *Iris orders flowers for me.*
Henry: *Of course she does. Get her a single rose.*
Dash: *Not a couple dozen?*
Henry: *One is plenty for her.*
Dash: *What color?*
Henry: *Use that brilliant brain of yours and figure that out for yourself. Time for my massage. Later.*
Henry: *One more thing. Don't ask her out via text. Call, or do it in person.*
Dash: *This isn't a date.*
Henry: *Trust me.*

Call? Dash hated talking on the phone. He got through conference calls when necessary, but he preferred communicating via text messages. Trust Henry? Dash supposed he could because Iris would be asleep when he arrived home and tomorrow, somebody would be around the house, either Tony,

Janice, or Leo—maybe all three.

Might as well do it now.

Dash pulled up her contact info. His finger hovered over the call button.

What was he waiting for?

This wasn't a date. He went out with his other friends and never should have stopped doing this with her.

Why had he?

They used to go out all the time. Dinner, movies, arcades at bowling alleys. They were out of the habit. It was as simple as that. Everything would be fine once they went out.

He jabbed his finger against the screen.

One ring, and Iris picked up.

"What's wrong?" She sounded breathless.

His pulse sputtered. "Why do you think something's wrong?"

"The last time you called me, Wes was in the hospital and not doing well."

The air in Dash's lungs whooshed out. That had been over two—closer to three—years ago. How had that happened?

"Dash?" she prompted.

Oh, right. "Do you have plans tomorrow night?"

"No. What do you need me to do?"

Dash gripped his phone. He hated that she thought he wanted her to do something for him. If only he could go back and do things over again. "Let's go to dinner."

"Out?" Her surprised tone cut sharply.

He would make this up to her. Somehow. "Yes."

Silence filled the line.

"I'd like that very much." Iris sounded like she was smiling.

Good, because so was he. "Anywhere special you'd like to go?"

"Wherever you want."

He'd expected her quick reply. At least he had a plan in mind. "I'll figure out something."

"Get back to work, or you'll be there too late. You don't want to be sleepy on the drive home."

He glanced at the futon where he'd spent many nights when he was tired. But her telling him that was typical. Iris had always looked out for him, even when they were younger. These days, his parents only cared about what he could give them, not him. "If I'm tired, I'll stay."

"Everything you need is in the cabinet closet, including a toiletry kit. I dropped off a new one last week."

He'd had no idea she was at his office. "What will I do without you?"

Dash cringed. He hadn't meant to say that aloud. The story of his life.

"Janice and Leo were with me, so they know what to do," Iris said in a cheery voice. "You'll be fine."

Probably, but it wouldn't be the same without her

there. Still, he wanted to reassure her. "I know you're right."

The husband and wife were in their fifties, both personable and skilled. The house was clean and organized, and Dash had no complaints. Even Tony was begrudgingly growing on Dash. The guy outdid himself with each meal, taking a favorite dish and adding something new to enhance it. His cookies were good, too. Though Iris's were better.

"In case I don't see you tonight or in the morning, I should be home around six tomorrow night and then we can go out to dinner."

"Sounds great." Her happiness seemed to flow from his phone's speaker and into him, wrapping around his heart and hugging tightly. "And remember…"

"Don't work too late," he finished for her. "I promise I won't."

"G'night."

"Sweet dreams." He disconnected from the call.

A feeling of contentment settled over him. Strange, given Iris was leaving and three new people now worked in his house. That kind of change should have had him jittery and freaking out.

But no complaints.

Dash just had to remember to buy her a flower. He set a reminder on his phone.

Done.

If only he could be home… He stared at his

monitor. Another hour and he would be. Then, he could concentrate on making sure Iris had a fun time at dinner.

And with him.

Chapter Ten

Thursday night, Iris threw a scarf on the floor outside her room. No matter how many times she'd watched the video from a social media influencer who could work magic with a piece of fabric, she couldn't tie it correctly to save her life.

She glanced at her reflection in the hall mirror. The dark jeans fit like a glove and were the most expensive clothing she owned. Whenever she wore them, she received compliments, which made them the perfect choice for tonight. She had no idea where they were eating—surprising because she was the one who made Dash's reservations—but in Portland, people dressed casually.

The coral sweater was pretty but plain. That was why she'd grabbed the scarf. She wanted to look nice for Dash.

Iris appreciated how he'd been spending time with her and texting her during the day to see how moving into her room had gone. What she couldn't understand was how different things felt between them. He'd played a starring role in her dreams, something that hadn't happened in almost a decade. And she kept finding him watching her.

Guess he was as glad to have her back in his life as she was to have him in hers.

She picked up the scarf and tied it per the video. This time, she looked as if she'd used a baby sling like Laurel Matthews wore as a fashion accessory.

"It's hopeless." Might as well admit defeat. "Maybe I should find something else to wear."

And she should probably stop talking to herself until she moved into her apartment.

"You look lovely." Janice climbed the stairs with a basket full of Dash's clothes.

Guess there would be no wandering around in a towel this week. Iris shook the thought from her head.

"What's the problem?" Janice asked.

"I can't tie the scarf right."

Janice set the laundry on the floor. "Let me try."

"Go for it." Iris handed over the scarf.

Before she could say anything, Janice folded and wrapped and circled Iris's neck until the scarf turned an average top into something worth a second look.

"Oh my." Iris stared at herself. "That's even better than what I was going for in the video. How did you do that?"

"For over ten years, Leo and I worked for a stylist in Los Angeles. I occasionally accompanied her to see clients, so I learned a few tricks along the way."

"Thanks for working your magic on me." Iris was afraid to touch the scarf because it was so perfect.

"You're welcome." Janice picked up the basket. "Where are you going on your date?"

"It's not a date. Just dinner with Dash."

"Tony will be heartbroken," Janice joked.

Iris laughed. Tony had cranked up the charm, but he appeared content with flirting. She was fine with that, too. Otherwise, turning him down could make things awkward with her living here. "Don't let him hear you say that. I think he prefers breaking hearts than having it done to his."

"I think you're correct." Janice glanced around as if to see if anyone was nearby. "You and Tony don't have any chemistry. Now, you and Dash… Yours is off the charts. Explosive."

"What? No. I mean." Iris took a breath to calm her heart rate. Chemistry and Dash were two things that needed to stay separate. "We're friends."

Janice studied her with curiosity. "Friendship is the best foundation for a relationship."

"It's not like that." Iris didn't want to give her the wrong idea. "I've known Dash since we were thirteen.

We're trying to rekindle our friendship. Nothing else."

"Well, I see the sparks between you. Leo does, too."

Heat pooled on her face. Iris didn't know what to say. "I…"

Janice hitched the basket to her left hip before touching Iris's shoulder. "Years ago, Leo and I worked for the same family. We were friends. More because of proximity than common interests, but we enjoyed eating our meals in the kitchen and occasionally did projects together. One day, I noticed his eyes were warm and bright. I realized how happy he made me when he said hello when we saw each other in the house. And I admitted to myself how hot he was."

Iris laughed, a combination of amusement and nerves. But she enjoyed hearing the story.

"The funny thing was, he was noticing things about me." Janice smiled softly. "I have no idea what caused the change between us. Maybe we were finally in a place where we could see each other more clearly. We tried being more than friends, and twenty-five years later we're still together."

"That's wonderful."

"It is. I'm grateful for each day with Leo." The love for her husband echoed in her eyes. "Don't get stuck on a label or how it's always been. Otherwise, you'll never experience the joy that falling in love with your friend brings. It's true magic."

Iris nodded, but love? All the reasons it wouldn't—couldn't—happen pounded in her brain.

The front door opened and then closed.

She inhaled sharply. That must be Dash.

A glance in the mirror had her smoothing her hair.

"For not a date, you're going to a lot of effort." Janice sounded amused.

"I don't go out much." Especially with him. This was about as close to a special occasion as Iris got. "I want to look nice."

"You do." Janice smiled. "Have fun."

"Thanks." Iris grabbed her jacket and purse from her room.

Walking down the stairs, her heart pounded against her rib cage. She kept hold of the railing, not knowing why she was suddenly nervous. It wasn't as if she hadn't eaten with Dash.

But this was new. She hoped it wouldn't be the last time they went out.

He stood at the entrance to the kitchen with his back to her. He wore khakis and a blue button-down shirt—he had a different pair for each day of the week.

"Hey." Her voice came out softer than she intended and not as steady as she'd wanted. "You're home early."

Facing her, he held a single coral-colored rose. The color was an exact match to her sweater. But that wasn't the thing that struck her the most.

As far as Iris knew, Dash had never given a woman flowers. Oh, he'd paid for them. Occasionally, ordering them had been his idea. But he'd never hand-delivered a rose or anything else.

Not until her.

That made her feel special, a way she wasn't used to feeling.

Dash extended the rose. "This is for you."

A thrill shot through Iris. With a tentative hand, she raised the bloom to her nose and sniffed the sweet fragrance. "It's beautiful. And the flower matches my shirt. Thanks."

Slow down or you'll be rambling soon.

She took a breath. "Let me put the flower in a vase."

As she went to the kitchen, Dash followed her. "I had no idea there were so many colors of roses. This one reminded me of you."

"We must have been on the same wavelength." She motioned to her sweater. "I appreciate the flower. It's been a long time since I've had any."

Ordering floral arrangements for Dash's house didn't count. She'd never thought to buy any for herself. That was something she would do differently at the apartment once she moved in. She grabbed a bud vase from a cabinet and filled it with water.

He bit his lip. "Are you out of the cottage?"

"I am." Iris placed the rose's stem into the water.

She would take the vase upstairs to her room later. "The place is clean. Janice and Leo move in tomorrow."

"Bittersweet?"

How did he know? "It's exactly that."

"Change is hard, but it's not all bad." Dash held her hand, lacing his fingers with hers. "Ready to go?"

Not trusting her voice, she nodded. Iris expected him to let go of her hand, but he didn't. The thrill she'd felt earlier morphed into hope.

Maybe Janice was right. Maybe something between them had shifted.

Would Iris get a taste of magic tonight?

She glanced at the rose on the counter. Maybe…

* * *

Iris sat across from Dash at her favorite fish restaurant. Every table was full, and the noise from customers kept getting louder. She didn't mind. This was the perfect date—make that night out. No matter what Janice might think and despite his holding Iris's hand on the way to the car—something she could get used to easily—this was nothing more than two friends eating dinner together.

And eat she had.

Sweet potato fries, clam chowder, and a fish taco. All three were delicious.

The best part was the easy flow of conversation.

From Dash telling her about the progress made with the beta testing for a new product and the recent success of a gaming team he sponsored, to Iris explaining what the culinary program would be like and the uniform she would wear.

He finished his salmon. "This restaurant is great. No wonder you like it so much."

"I do." Tonight, though, ranked as her favorite visit. This wasn't a fancy or expensive place. They talked about everyday things. But Iris couldn't remember the last time she'd felt this content. "How did you know to bring me here?"

He wiped his mouth with a napkin. "I asked Henry."

She struggled to understand when Dash had been her friend for over fifteen years. "Why him? We only got to know each other over the holidays."

Dash shrugged. "Seemed like the best person after you did things together during your staycation. I wasn't sure if you'd gone out with Tony."

"I haven't." The words burst from her mouth. The guy was a wonderful chef who understood Dash's eating quirks, but she didn't want to date him. Not that he'd asked. Yet. But she hoped he never did. As she mentioned to Janice, that would be too awkward. "Though Tony knows most of the best restaurants in town."

"So do I," Dash said in a slightly annoyed tone. "But I wanted to know your favorites."

She sipped her iced tea. "You succeeded."

"Thanks, but I'm sure Henry will want all the credit."

Dash's grin brightened his face. He really was handsome. More so now that he'd grown into his height and features. His blue shirt intensified his eyes, turning them a cornflower blue and making them pop.

She took another drink.

The server, a young woman dressed in a T-shirt and jeans, placed the bill folder on the table and removed their plates.

Dash placed a credit card inside. "I've enjoyed spending time with you this week."

"Same, and I admit it's great to get out of the house. Not that there's anything wrong with being there, but it's big—"

"And lonely." His mouth twisting, he stared at his nearly empty plate.

Uh-oh. This wasn't good. "Dash?"

He looked up with a pained expression. "I'm sorry for not being a better friend. Even when we did stuff—which wasn't as often as I thought—it was at the house. We never went out like this. I remember you asking me to do things with you, but then you stopped. Why?"

"You really want to know?" She didn't think he would.

"Yes."

Okay. Here goes. "If you'd said no once or twice, I wouldn't have stopped asking. I didn't until the sixth no. After that, there was no reason to ask again."

"I didn't realize…" He hung his head before rubbing his chest. "There's no excuse."

"You had your company, women you were dating, and the guys."

Dash raised his chin. "Who did you have?"

"A few friends." Four, if Iris wanted to be specific, but he was hurting. She didn't want to add to that. "Let's forget about the past. We're out now and should make the most of it."

He exhaled loudly. "You're right, which proves how smart you are."

"Yeah, right." She laughed. "You've made billions from your gray matter. Me? I still don't understand calculus. I would have failed that class and never graduated without you."

A corner of his mouth slanted upward. "Have you ever used calculus in your daily life?"

She grimaced. "Never. Thank goodness."

"Then who cares if you got it or not? That's one subject, and book smart differs from life smart. Sometimes I wish I had more of the latter."

"You have both."

"Not in equal percentages. And before you say otherwise, you know it's true."

She did, so she ran her fingers across her lips to zip them.

It was his turn to laugh.

The server grabbed the bill. "I'll be right back with your receipt."

Dash stretched out his legs. "I'm having people over on Sunday to watch the playoff games. I'd like for you to be there. I promise, no calculus required."

"Oh, okay." Iris had recipes that worked well with his or his friends' football game parties. She would theme the food menu to the two teams playing and their cities. "I'll speak with Tony—"

"He's available," Dash interrupted. "I asked him yesterday to see if he could work."

Iris let the words sink in. This was… She didn't know what to say. "You're adjusting faster to the new staff than I thought you would."

Dash's intense gaze met hers, but then he shrugged. "It's not like I have a choice. And you picked excellent replacements."

True, but she bristled. He should have come to her first. She was the one who took care of things for him and…

Ridiculous.

She was being utterly ridiculous.

Iris wanted the transition to be smooth for him. She'd hired good people to take her place so that would happen. His going to Tony meant she'd succeeded. That was a good thing. Yet, it felt…strange, and she didn't like it.

Dash reached across the table and covered her

hand with his. "Hey, you okay?"

She nodded. "I'm happy things are working out so well."

"I'll never be happy you're leaving." His thumb rubbed her hand. "But I know this is what you want to do. And I'm glad we're hanging out again."

Hanging out.

The two words reverberated through her. That sounded so friend-like, but his hand was still on top of hers. His eyes focused on Iris, as if she were the only person in the place, making her feel like this dinner was so much more than two friends out to eat.

Stop.

She'd made this mistake when they were younger.

All she'd ended up doing was falling hard and winding up heartbroken.

Maybe in the past three years with the various women he'd dated, he'd become more touchy-feely. That was the most logical explanation. Given he was a tech guy and ruled by logic, the most likely reason, too.

What happened with Janice and Leo to bring them together wasn't happening with her and Dash. Maybe somewhere deep inside Iris wished it would, but she needed to be practical and squash the desire before it grew any bigger.

She pulled her hand from beneath his. "Me, too."

He nodded. "So on Sunday, I want you there."

"I'll be there helping Tony."

"I don't want you working in the kitchen." Dash scratched his chin. "I want you watching the game with us."

Us.

His friends.

Henry, Blaise, and Hadley had been so welcoming to her at Christmastime. Brett had been helpful with her budgeting, and Laurel provided the names of inexpensive consignment stores where Iris might find furniture for the apartment. The others treated her nicely during their events she worked. The only problem? They were billionaires. So was Dash, but he was still the geek he'd always been. He just had more money now to buy cool stuff.

What would she say to his friends?

Hey, how are you? I'm staying in the guest bedroom for free and driving one of Dash's cars until I can move into my tiny apartment that costs less than your monthly coffee bill.

No way. She may have opened up to Henry, and Brett and Laurel had needed to know her situation to help, but no more until she was on her feet and thriving. "Thanks, but—"

"Please." He leaned forward with a hopeful gleam in his eyes. "It would mean a lot to me. You could also see how Tony does."

"He handled Saturday night dinner crowds with ease. A football watch party will be a cinch for him."

"Then you can relax and enjoy yourself."

The server returned the folder. Dash put his

credit card into his wallet and signed the bill.

Relaxing and enjoying herself would be impossible if she was nervous. And she would be. Working an event was one thing. She'd never been a guest at something like that. A good thing she had the perfect excuse. "I start school the next day."

"You don't have to stay the entire time," Dash countered. "And you need to eat."

Iris had a feeling he would come up with a reason to counter any excuse. At least he hadn't brought out the puppy dog eyes. "Okay, I will be there. I'm not promising how long."

A sly smile slid across his face. "That's fine with me. Who knows? You might decide you're having fun."

"I might." But Iris doubted it. Still, *hanging out* more with Dash would be nice. "But no promises."

"Do you want to do anything else?"

She glanced out the window. It wasn't raining, per se, but appeared misty and cold. "I'd suggest a walk along the waterfront, but not in this weather. I want to be one hundred percent healthy for the first day of class."

He scooted his chair away from the table. "Then let's get you home."

She stood and shrugged on her coat. Dash followed her outside.

The drive was silent except for the music streaming, but the quiet wasn't uncomfortable. It was nice to be in the same space as him.

When they entered the house through the garage, he placed his hand at the small of her back to escort her inside. Even with the layers of clothing separating his skin from hers, warmth emanated at the spot of contact.

That told her she needed a reality check. And fast. Getting caught up in a personal fairy tale would only hurt her.

"Do you want to watch a show?" Dash asked. "We could pick a sitcom. Something short."

Yes, which meant she should say no. Her head was all mixed up about Dash. "I have a few things to put away, and I need to get to bed early. We checked off everything that's usually done on Thursdays and Fridays today so I could help Janice and Leo move in the cottage tomorrow."

"Then I'll say good night now."

As he leaned closer, she turned her head to look at him. His lips brushed hers.

The contact was light, but she felt a shock followed by a blast of warmth.

Dash jerked back, appearing startled. He blinked. "Uh, sorry. I was aiming for your cheek."

"Th-that's okay." The way her lips tingled after the brief peck wasn't anywhere close to being okay.

His Adam's apple bobbed. "Good night."

Eager to put distance between them, Iris nodded and then headed for the stairs, fighting the urge to touch her lips. As fast as she could without falling on her face, she hurried to the second floor. She entered her room and closed the door behind her.

If she hadn't turned her head, he would have kissed her cheek.

But why would he kiss her at all?

That was what Henry did, not Dash.

And the worst part, the brief peck left her wanting more.

Iris touched her lips.

What is happening? And how would she survive staying here until her apartment was ready if a brush of Dash's lips could make her swoon?

This is bad.

Bad, bad, bad.

Chapter Eleven

After tossing and turning in bed for ten minutes, Dash gave up on sleep. He sat and grabbed his Nintendo Switch from the nightstand. Maybe playing a game would quiet his out-of-control brain so he could rest for a few hours. Otherwise, he would keep replaying what happened downstairs with Iris.

And her soft, pink lips.

An IED obliterated his avatar.

Okay, he shouldn't have been thinking about her. Or the smile that kept igniting a flame inside him whenever it was directed his way. Or how he wished—

The enemy took him out. Man, he didn't know he could be shot that many times.

Gaming wasn't working. He was still thinking

about Iris.

Dash tossed the handheld console onto the mattress. Maybe TV would distract him.

Pressing a button on the remote turned on the television set. A hockey game played. He wasn't a huge fan, but all he needed was something to take his mind off Iris. He arranged a pillow behind his back.

A right wing stole the puck before a defenseman skated close, nearly checking him into the boards. The puck was passed to the center. The player took a shot but missed the net by mere inches. The player's frustration showed on his face and how he clutched his stick.

Dash snickered. "Know exactly how you feel, buddy."

Going out to dinner with Iris had been like time traveling to when they'd been best friends and did everything together. Not in high school. All the way back to middle school when he couldn't stop thinking how pretty she was and how much he liked touching her hand.

Loser.

How had he managed to go out with a woman more than once when he was acting like a thirteen-year-old with Iris?

Maybe his nickname Wonderkid, emphasis on the last syllable, was truer than not. Or maybe, Iris was the reason.

Cheers sounded from the television, but he

ignored the players skating back and forth.

Dash never meant to kiss her on the lips. One hundred percent true, he'd been going for her cheek—the way friends did.

Or at least Henry did.

Dash hadn't expected she'd turn her head toward him at the right—or rather, wrong—time. No one could have anticipated that. It was his luck.

Both good and bad.

The brush of his lips against her soft ones had been, in a word, awesome, and he'd wanted nothing more than to kiss her longer, but he pulled away because he hadn't asked if he could kiss her.

A buzzer sounded.

He startled.

A glance at the television showed players leaving the ice. The period must be over. So much for the game distracting him.

The kiss had lasted maybe a second, but Dash couldn't stop thinking about it or her. He couldn't decide if she was surprised or upset. The way she'd bolted upstairs reminded him of a thoroughbred in the Kentucky Derby on the final straightaway.

If Iris had stayed, would she have told him what she was thinking? If she wanted another kiss?

Dash did, because one taste, barely a hint, made him want more. But how would that work when they were friends?

Friends.

He mulled over the word.

It had only been one week, but he felt closer to Iris than he had to Raina or any girlfriend before her. Okay, he'd known Iris for over fifteen years. They'd lived together, either in the same apartment or on the same property for the past six. Other friends joked the reason he hadn't been interested in marriage was he already had a wife—Iris—just without the other…benefits.

If that were true, he'd been a horrible husband, taking her for granted and ignoring her needs. Not even married and he was following in his parents' footsteps.

He half laughed.

Only it wasn't funny.

Dash slouched.

Once Iris moved out, things would change. He tried to imagine what that would look like. Going out to dinner. Watching a movie. Hanging out.

None of that seemed…enough…after tonight. But what did that mean in real life—friends to best friends to…girlfriend and boyfriend?

That would be…

Wonderful.

No, risky.

Too much?

Iris wanted a happily ever after. The only thing he believed in was happy for now, and that was on a good day.

Was a compromise even possible?

Dash had more questions than answers. He hadn't been willing to try being more than friends when they were younger. How was their situation different now? If anything, their friendship was in a worse position, nowhere as strong as it had been in the past.

His fault, completely. He'd been stupid and selfish. He didn't deserve another chance, but Iris was giving him one. Focusing on rebuilding their friendship should be the only thing on his mind, not where they might go in the future. He didn't want to ruin things between them again. Had he already?

Dash dragged his hand through his hair. He'd apologized for the mis-aimed kiss earlier, but was that enough?

Could he have messed everything up by accident? Not knowing would keep him awake all night.

He glanced at the time. Ten o'clock. It wasn't too late. He would see if she was asleep and then decide what to do.

Dash jumped out of bed and headed to the door.
Wait.

He jolted to a stop. Going to see her without wearing a shirt might be skirting their rules. He was taking no chances.

Grabbing a T-shirt from his dresser remedied that. He put it on, not caring if it clashed with his plaid sleep pants. He was clothed, not in his underwear or a towel. He was good per their rules.

Dash went to her room, his steps not as confident as he'd hoped they would be. No light shone from beneath Iris's door. He listened but heard nothing.

Leave it until morning.

He would if he could, but maybe Iris was feeling the same way as him and unable to sleep, too.

Just get it over with.

Dash tapped a knuckle lightly against the door.

"Is someone there?" Iris asked, her voice soft.

His stomach fluttered. Butterflies or nausea? He couldn't tell. "It's me. I mean, Dash."

Idiot.

You and she are the only two in the house.

"Come in," she said.

His muscles twitched. A desire to flee overcame him.

Pull yourself together, Cabot.

As Dash gripped the knob, he took a fortifying breath and opened the door.

The room was dark except for the glow of an eReader screen on Iris's lap. She sat in bed with her back supported by pillows against the headboard. She wore long-sleeved fleece pajamas. One foot poked out from under the comforter.

He forced a smile. "I wasn't sure if you'd be awake."

"I couldn't sleep."

"Me, either." Wanting to talk to Iris like this was

out of his comfort zone. Normally, he was the peacemaker, who never brought up difficult or uncomfortable topics. He disliked conflict to the nth degree. Maybe that was why he hadn't a clue how to begin. But she was worth getting over himself to talk to her.

As she raised her eReader, the screen cast shadows on her face. "I've been reading."

"I was watching a hockey game. Well, trying." He scrubbed his face, struggling for what to say next. "I apologized, but it's still bugging me. I meant to kiss you on the cheek, but then you turned your head. Not that I minded kissing your lips."

Ugh. All that money in the bank, yet he was beyond help. Rambling. Acting foolish.

"It's okay, Dash." Iris sat straighter. "You didn't do that on purpose."

"Thanks." A weight lifted. "All this crazy stuff was streaming through my brain, and it wouldn't stop. I was sure I'd messed up again, and you wouldn't want to be friends."

Would you shut up?

He bit his bottom lip to keep from talking.

"You didn't mess anything up, but…" Her mouth quirked. "In all the years I've known you, you've never kissed me goodbye. Why did you tonight?"

Dash shrugged. That wasn't an answer, but the thought of saying the words aloud made him wish he hadn't eaten so much tonight.

"Not good enough." Her voice was firmer. "Use words."

Talking to a conference room full of investors or tech-junkies was easier than standing in front of Iris. She deserved an answer. Still, he shifted his weight between his bare feet.

He took a breath. And another. "Sometimes I can't believe you're giving our friendship another go after what I did or didn't do. I keep wanting to touch you to make sure you're real. Here. Tonight, I kissed you because that's what Henry does with you and you are friends with him. Weird, huh?"

Her smile reached all the way to her eyes. "It's sweet."

"I want to do better with you. Though I'm not as smooth as Henry."

Not even close, but Dash kept that to himself.

"You weren't unsmooth if that helps," she offered. "The problem was, I turned my head."

"Yes, but that was like having second dessert."

Iris laughed. "We never had a first one, but I know what you mean."

Now, that was interesting and gave him an idea. "Do you mind?"

"What?"

He wanted to tread carefully around Iris. But he couldn't deny wanting another kiss, even as friends. The screen's glow made her look more like an actress from an old movie.

Beautiful.

But her looks weren't her biggest appeal. It was her heart, one that gave and cared. One that had so much love to give to the right person. Dash swallowed.

"What did you mean?" she prompted.

"The touching, holding hands, kisses." The words rushed from his mouth one after another like the water cascading from Multnomah Falls after snowmelt runoff.

"I'm not used to it, but I *could* get used to it, Dash."

Good. He blew out the breath he'd been holding.

She eyed him warily. "How about you?"

"Same." And this was where it got tricky, because he wouldn't mind kissing her right now. Probably not a good idea. That didn't stop him from taking a step closer to the side of her bed. "Do you think we need to add rules about those things? Like asking permission?"

That seemed a no-brainer so that he didn't repeat what happened tonight.

Iris shrugged. "Holding hands isn't a big deal."

Except it felt like one to Dash.

"Henry doesn't do that with his kisses," she added. "If it's just a greeting or farewell kiss between friends, that might be overkill."

His throat constricted.

"If it was something else? Between friends?" *Ugh.*

Dash *had* said that aloud. "Hypothetically."

Iris tilted her chin. "Hypothetically, asking would be polite if it was more than a casual hello or goodbye."

"Makes sense."

"Anything else?"

It was too soon for a good night kiss. What they'd discussed was enough for tonight.

"I'm good." But he wanted to say something else. "I'm happy you're staying here."

"Me, too." She placed her eReader on the nightstand and then reached out to touch the top of his hand. "I'm here until the first. I'm not going to just disappear."

He nodded.

"And after I move into my apartment, I'm just a text or a call away." She squeezed his hand. "Living in different places doesn't mean we'll never see each other again. I want us to be friends."

Dash relished her touch. Her skin was warm, but he didn't need a light to see the calluses and scars on her hand. A hand that cooked and baked and cared for him. A hand he wanted to hold on to tightly and not let go. "Me, too."

"Who knows?" A closed-mouth smile spread. "We might see each other more."

"I hope so."

"Me, too." She let go of him, and he wished she hadn't. "We should try and sleep, or tomorrow could be rough."

"Yeah, I can't afford to be a zombie."

"A diet of caffeine and sugar can only do so much," she joked.

"Especially while testing a prototype." His company was planning to launch a product in a new industry by Q3 at the latest. This was a pet project from the research lab he'd set up last year. No one but the small team knew about it, but the impact and results could be enormous. "Depending on how things go, I may sleep in my office tomorrow night to get an early start on Saturday morning's tests."

"Good luck. I have plans on Saturday."

Jealousy flared, but he kept himself from asking what she was doing and with whom. As her friend, it was none of his business. Even if he wanted to know her plans.

"So, I'll see you on Sunday," she added.

Watching football with his friends. Funny, but he'd rather be spending time alone with her. "See you then."

He only hoped the next three days passed quickly because he was already missing her.

**

Sunday, the pregame show was almost over. Dash stood in the great room where he had a good view of everything. Adam and Cambria refilled their glasses at the bar. Kieran, Mason, and Blaise stood by the buffet table near the kitchen. Brett, Laurel, and Henry cooed over little Noelle in the corner. Wes, Paige, Selah, and Rachael sat talking. Everyone appeared to be in place except for Iris.

Kickoff wasn't until 12:05, but Dash thought she would have reappeared by now after helping Tony prepare the food and set up the buffet.

Where was she?

Dash checked the time on his phone again. Only a couple of minutes had passed since the last time he looked.

"When did you become a clock watcher?" Blaise asked, holding a beer bottle.

"I'm not." Dash glanced around the room again. "Just checking to see if everyone who should be here is."

"They are."

Except for Iris. Wait. Someone else was missing. "Where's Hadley?"

"Upstairs with Iris."

Oh, so maybe she wasn't avoiding the party. He snagged his soda from the end table and drank. Normally, he would have beer, but he didn't need to get buzzed or drunk tonight with Iris around.

Blaise took a sip of beer before tilting his head at Tony. "The new guy working out?"

"He's an excellent chef."

"Still, no Iris."

"Did you taste the BBQ?" Dash asked. "It's some of the best I've had."

"It's not bad," Blaise admitted. "But where are the pulled pork sliders?"

Someone laughed—Wes. The women must be keeping him entertained.

"Tony came up with the menu." Truthfully, Dash missed the sliders, too. But he'd wanted to see what Tony came up with on his own. "You won't go hungry."

"That's true." Blaise leaned closer and lowered his voice. "Just make sure Iris gives Tony the slider recipe."

Dash laughed. "Will do."

Blaise's face brightened. "And there's my lovely wife and Iris."

As Iris came toward Dash, his breath caught in his throat. She wore a pair of jeans with a long-sleeved shirt. Her hair was in a ponytail, which was typical when she cooked, only she wasn't wearing the apron she'd had on earlier.

His heart pitter-pattered in a way it hadn't before.

Not the reaction he was expecting.

He rocked back on his heels, trying to look cool, when his temperature had shot up ten degrees in the last two seconds.

He gulped from his soda can.

Hadley slid next to Blaise. "Iris gave me the recipe for her famous sliders, so you can stop grumbling."

Blaise made a face. "I wasn't—"

"Yes, you were," Dash joked, trying to downplay his sweaty palms. He wiped one on his jeans, transferred his drink into that hand, and then brushed his other hand on his thigh.

Hadley kissed Blaise's cheek. "It doesn't matter because now you can have sliders whenever you want."

"Thanks, Iris." Blaise put his arm around Hadley. "We owe you."

Iris smiled. "I'm always happy to help."

Was she? Because her smile looked forced. She also kept toying with the edge of her shirt. Dash didn't like how uncomfortable she appeared when today was supposed to be fun.

"Glad to hear that." Hadley beamed. "And I hope you'll help me out."

"Uh-oh." Blaise laughed. "What are you planning now?"

"Matchmaking world domination." Hadley did a dab, mimicking a play they'd shown on the pregame show. "What can I say except Iris is the perfect match for a new client."

Wait a minute. Dash focused on Hadley. "Match?"

Hadley's grin suggested she knew a secret. "As soon as I met this guy, I thought of Iris."

No way. Dash had just gotten his friend back. He didn't want to share her with some guy she was dating.

Uh-oh. Hadley was known as the wife finder. Her client was probably looking for more than a girlfriend. And if he hit it off with Iris…

A pressure built in Dash's chest.

"That's why you're the best at what you do despite Henry's claims." Blaise beamed with pride at his wife before looking at Iris. "Being talked into doing that questionnaire on Christmas could turn into something, after all."

Blushing, Iris shrugged.

Dash remembered the many pages of questions he'd answered for Hadley. "You filled one out?"

"Of course she did," Hadley answered before Iris could. "Well, after I talked her into it. I didn't have anyone in mind for her then, but I had a feeling it was only a matter of time."

A matter of time before some guy, most likely a wealthy one because Hadley wasn't cheap, swept Iris off her feet and took her away to live happily ever after.

He forced himself to breathe. "What about culinary school?"

"That's my focus right now," Iris said without a hint of uncertainty. "Hadley knows that."

The matchmaker nodded. "I'm aware of your priorities, but one date won't hurt."

Dash wasn't so sure about that. He and Wes had each agreed to go on one date. That was all Wes went on, but not Dash. He'd dated Raina for months. That meant one date could turn into another for Iris.

Whether culinary school was important or not, she could be wearing a diamond engagement ring before she graduated.

His heart palpitated.

Iris touched his arm. "You okay?"

No, but he didn't want to worry her. "I'm fine."

Dash didn't like being jealous, but he'd gotten used to it. The sense of dread building inside him, however, was new. He didn't like that at all.

"Could you give me a hand, Iris?" Tony asked, standing in front of the stove.

Iris's concerned gaze met Dash's. "If you need me…"

Dash would always need her. To what extent, however, was something he needed to figure out. "Go help Tony."

"I'll talk to you later," Iris said to Hadley and Blaise before rounding the island to help the chef.

Blaise's eyes darkened. "What's wrong?"

Hadley glanced at the kitchen. "Is something going on between you and Iris?"

"I'm not sure," Dash admitted. "We're friends. Well, working on it. But please don't set her up with that client yet. Not until I—we—figure this out."

Chapter Twelve

The second game ended with cheers and boos, since people were split on which team they supported, but no one wanted to stick around to see the post-game interviews and trophy presentation. Dash accomp-anied his friends out to their cars, leaving only Iris and Tony inside.

From chaos to quiet in a matter of minutes.

Iris didn't mind at all.

Water flowed from the kitchen faucet where Tony washed a pot. His apron was wet, and sweat gleamed on his skin. Nice eye candy, but he was definitely the look-don't-touch type. She had to admit he'd been completely professional today. He'd toned down his flirting with female guests and worked hard. He looked like he needed a shower, a cold drink, and then sleep. Not in that particular order.

Iris carried glasses from the great room. "Fantastic job. You put together a wonderful menu, but my favorites were the crab appetizers you made for the second game. Mouthwatering good and clever use of puff pastry sheets."

"Thanks." As he rinsed the pot, more water splattered on his apron. Tony laughed. "I'm out of practice washing everything myself."

She set the cups on the counter. "It's not like a restaurant."

"No, but I'm enjoying this. And I love the hours." He turned off the water. "I appreciated having you for backup today."

"Happy to help."

Tony dried his hands. "I can't believe you did these parties on your own."

She shrugged. "They get easier, but you can hire extra help. Dash doesn't mind. I did that with the bigger events, especially the annual New Year's Eve party when you need bartenders and servers. I also catered the desserts so I could focus on the food."

"Smart."

"It's all in the binder." Iris had made three of them—one for Tony, Janice, and Leo. Each detailed their areas of responsibility.

"Does it include your pulled pork slider recipe? More than one person asked if I'd made them."

She laughed. "I'll put a copy in there. Today was

THE DEAL BREAKER

your show, and it was a smash hit."

His chest puffed. "Now I just need to hear what the boss man says."

"Trust me," she reassured him. "Dash is pleased."

Tony's face lit up, his dimples deepening. "That's what matters most."

It was. Iris was relieved Dash would be in good hands. That had been her goal when she interviewed applicants.

"I'll see what else is left in the great room." She grabbed a cloth, went in the living area, and wiped off an end table. Thankfully, football and poker games didn't leave a big mess. Nothing like the larger functions.

"You don't have to clean up." Dash stood between the kitchen and great room with his arms crossed. Not smiling, he came toward her. "You're a guest."

"That doesn't mean I can't help." As she wiped another end table, she lowered her voice. "Tony's been on his feet all day. He doesn't need to do this, too."

"You used to do it."

"That's why I know how tiring these parties are," she said in a matter-of-fact tone, not wanting to argue about this. "Especially your first one."

Dash's brows wrinkled. "You never mentioned it."

Iris shrugged. She'd learned to handle everything

herself, but others wouldn't have the same drive to care for Dash as she had.

"I got used to it." She ran the rag over the coffee table. "That's why having more people on staff, each with their own area of expertise, will be more efficient. Janice will be Tony's backup, cooking for you when he's off."

Dash lowered his arms to his sides. "You figured out the best way for it to work."

She'd tried. "Spreading the work around makes sense."

"If I'd hired more staff to help you—"

"I'd still be returning to culinary school." Something Iris should have done as soon as she'd saved enough to cover tuition and rent. Better late than never. "If not now, then later."

"Good to know."

Seeing him accept what she was doing made her happy.

She studied the great room, checking to see if she'd missed anything. She straightened a throw pillow on the couch. "Janice will vacuum and mop tomorrow. That's what I did."

"I never noticed what you did. The house was just clean."

Satisfaction flowed through Iris. She pushed back her shoulders. "Then I did my job right."

"Not if you were overworked," he countered.

"That only happened at the beginning. I adapted

quickly." She glanced at the kitchen, where Tony put away pans. "Oh, I almost forgot. I'm giving him my slider recipe."

That brought a welcome smile to Dash's face. "Blaise will be thrilled."

"You?"

He nodded. "Yours are the best, but this will keep my friends happy."

The compliment buoyed her spirits. No one was irreplaceable, and she was sad about leaving, but she didn't want these six years to be forgotten. Not that Dash would. At least she hoped not.

Dash went over to Tony, who had removed his apron.

"Thanks for today. You did a great job." Dash handed the chef something. "Go home and relax."

Tony stared at the money in his palm with a goofy grin on his face. "Thank you. And I will."

Holding his apron and dish towels, Tony came toward her. "Have a great first day tomorrow."

"I will." She took the laundry from him. "Get out of here."

He leaned closer and whispered, "You never mentioned tips."

"Surprise!" She hadn't mentioned the special "bonuses" she'd occasionally received.

"I love my new job." With that, Tony strutted to the front door.

Iris dumped the items in the laundry room for

Janice to wash tomorrow.

When she returned to the great room, Dash sat on the couch. His legs were crossed at the ankles. Two beer bottles sat on the coffee table. "Join me."

The invitation was unexpected, but welcome. She sat next to him. "You didn't drink any alcohol today."

Dash's head jerked back. "I didn't think anyone noticed."

"It's my job to notice stuff." That was why Iris was good at anticipating his needs. She hadn't been able to train her replacements to do that yet, but she hoped in time, they would figure it out as she had.

"I noticed you ate food but skipped the desserts." He picked up his beer before fixing his gaze on her. "That's not your usual MO."

She shrugged, not wanting to tell him the real reason. "I wasn't hungry."

Not a lie. She hadn't needed more food.

"I've seen you eat sweets after a big meal." His lips pursed. "Tell me why."

Iris took a drink. The pale ale tasted good.

"Iris."

She picked at a corner of the label. "It's nothing."

"Then tell me." His firm voice told her he wouldn't let this drop.

Unfortunately. Iris blew out a breath. "The desserts were popular with your friends. I wanted to make sure everyone had enough."

He groaned. "You were a guest."

"It's hard to see myself that way when I've always worked here." The words rushed out before she could stop them. "I also want Tony to succeed at this job. That means impressing your friends so they hire him to work private parties."

Dash rose, went into the kitchen, and opened the refrigerator.

"Do you want me to make you something to eat?" she called out to him.

"No. You've done enough."

That sounded ominous. "What are you doing?"

"Found it." He returned with a plastic container, removed the lid, and held out the contents—Tony's leftover desserts—to her. "Have one."

"Bossy."

"You do the same to me," Dash said a beat later.

Okay, he was right. She took a pink-colored mousse in a chocolate cup with a peppermint swirl candy on top. She studied the color and consistency before biting into it. The peppermint filled her mouth, followed by a more bitter chocolate flavor. The combination worked well together. Iris swallowed. "Delicious. Thank you."

He pushed the container toward her. "Have another."

"I'm good. Thanks."

Dash set the container on the table and then leaned back. "Did you have fun today?"

"Yes." She'd enjoyed herself more than she

thought she would. "The games were good."

He studied her as if she were data which his company mined. "You were quiet."

She wasn't used to him noticing her. *Be careful what you wish for.* "I usually am."

"Not with me."

"What can I say?" Iris joked. "You bring me out of my shell."

"I want you to feel comfortable around them." Concern sounded in his voice and shown on his face. "I don't think you were. Not the entire time."

Guess he was changing because he usually wasn't so perceptive. At least, not with her. "I tried, but I'm used to serving, not being served. I kept wanting to refill glasses and pick up plates. That's who I am."

"It is. And you're good at it." He put his arm on the top of the couch and angled toward her. "It'll get easier the next time."

She gulped. "Next time?"

"Watching the Super Bowl at Kieran's house." Dash's face practically glowed. "I want you to come with me."

That was unexpected. Iris understood being invited because she was staying here. That was the polite thing to do, but going to someone else's house seemed odd. He'd never asked her to do that.

She wondered if this invitation was out of politeness or pity. She hoped not the latter. "I move into my apartment on the first, so I won't be staying here."

"So?" He spoke as if it wasn't a big deal, which confused her more. "Friends hang out."

Friends did that, but she hadn't told him the other reason she hadn't been comfortable today. Being in the kitchen cooking and keeping the buffet full meant she socialized little. Watching the game with his friends, seeing the happy couples with their touches, kisses, and glances, had made her want that, too.

In ways she hadn't wanted in a long time—years.

Weird when she was about to make her dream of finishing culinary school a reality.

"Yes, but…" She peeled more of the label off the bottle.

Dash took the beer from her hand and set it on the table. "Please talk to me."

She hunched her shoulders. "It's embarrassing?"

"Given I've made a fool of myself in front of you at least a hundred times more, this will even the score a little." His voice was lighthearted and playful.

She appreciated that. Now, it was her turn. "I don't think I want to spend another day with so many couples who are madly in love. They are nice, and the PDA isn't off the chart, but it reminds me what's missing from my life. Why do that to myself?"

Dash leaned toward her, his arm falling around her. "Is that what you want?"

Iris sighed, as if exhaling her hopes and dreams could make them come true. "I've always wanted that in one form or another. Happily ever after, remember?"

He nodded. "Is that why you filled out Hadley's questionnaire? So you can date?"

Huh? She scrunched her nose. "I date."

His mouth slanted. "You do?"

Did Dash not realize where she'd been on her days off? Given how little they talked, probably not. "I do."

His eyebrows drew together. "Who?"

"There have been a few guys over the years. Nothing too serious. I thought one might turn into more, but things ended after a couple months."

He cleared his throat. "What happened?"

"Will's work transferred him to Raleigh, North Carolina." Keeping her voice steady was easy because she hadn't been in love. Besides, she wouldn't have left Dash in Portland to move somewhere else. "He didn't ask me to go, and I didn't offer. End of story."

Dash opened his mouth before closing it. He tried again. "I had no idea."

"You had no reason to know." She didn't blame him. "You never asked, and we weren't exactly buddy-buddy then. I made sure our dates didn't interfere with what you needed."

That had been an issue with one guy, which was probably why Royce had ghosted her after three dates.

Dash scooted closer. "What else don't I know about you?"

His body pressed against her, raising her

temperature twenty degrees. She fought the urge to fan herself, but that would be a dead giveaway as to the effect he had on her. "I don't know."

"Come on," he urged. "I feel as if I'm missing a three-year chunk of your life, but I bet you could tell me everything I did for the past three years."

"You would win that bet because I do know what you did. Don't forget, I kept your calendar, made dinner reservations for your dates, and sent flowers or gifts as required."

"At least I knew that about you," he teased.

She nodded, chewing the inside of her mouth. "Janice is all set to help you there."

"I don't want to talk about my new housekeeper," he said quickly. "I want you to tell me. One thing."

Iris had one. A big one. *Should I tell him*? Only two other people knew, Henry being one of them.

Iris twisted away from him so she faced forward.

Once upon a time, even a few years ago, Iris wouldn't have hesitated. She'd found out at Christmastime, and it wasn't something to tell a boss. This was a conversation to share with a good friend.

A close friend.

Dash?

"Hey." He squeezed her shoulder. "I'm committed to strengthening our friendship. I realize those are just words, but they're true. Please believe me."

Seven days didn't make up for all those years, but

Dash was making an effort. They were better off than they'd been a week ago when she could have never imagined herself sitting here with him like this. "I do."

Friendship was a two-way street. It wasn't as tenuous as say a romance, but both friends needed to do their part so their relationship thrived. She would do hers.

After some liquid courage.

Iris drank from the bottle. She took one more sip before placing her beer on the coffee table. "I found my dad."

Dash gasped. "How? When? Did you speak with him?"

She should have expected the blast of questions as if this were a press conference. Though he was the one usually answering them. "Henry did everything. He hired a private investigator in December. Surprisingly, it didn't take long to receive the info."

Dash's face went slack. He blinked slowly. "I never thought… I should have done that for you."

It was her turn to reassure him. "Your parents may be raving lunatics, but they're alive and in your life—albeit like parasites."

A vein ticked at his jaw. "Bloodsucking, or rather, money-burning ones."

"Henry's parents are dead." Dash knew this, but she wanted him to understand how this happened. "He brought it up when we were waiting for the train at Zoolights. His offer stunned me, but to be honest, a part of me wondered what happened to my dad. If he was alive, happy, missing me."

Dash swallowed. "I'm glad Henry could do that for you."

She blew out a breath. "Though after what I found out, I almost wish I hadn't said yes."

Dash's gaze locked on Iris. His hand tightened on her. "Is your dad okay?"

"He's fine. Running a new restaurant in Boise, Idaho."

Only a state away, but the distance didn't matter much. He'd proven what kind of man he was when he left Portland, but the information the PI discovered confirmed that and more.

"That's good, right?" His tone was uncertain.

"My dad married his online girlfriend. I knew she was younger, but I found out her exact age. She's four years older than me. I also discovered I'm no longer an only child." Iris couldn't keep the sarcasm from her voice. "I have a seven-year-old half brother and a five-year-old half sister."

Dash's brows shot up. "Seven? Your mom died six years ago."

Iris hung her head. The truth hurt, cutting deep. Oh, her father had already knocked himself off his pedestal when he'd left her, but this… He'd done this to her mom, too.

She blew out a shaky breath. "My father cheated on my mom while she was sick. As she lay dying, he was making plans to join his mistress and son. The nights I worked at the restaurant, I don't think he spent the entire time with my mom. He couldn't have if he had another family nearby. Everything he said—did—was a lie." Iris's voice cracked, and her eyes stung.

"I'm so sorry." The sincerity in Dash's voice covered her like a fleece blanket. He put his arm around her. "I thought what he originally did to you was bad. Now this…"

"There aren't any words." She leaned into Dash, grateful for his support. "I believed he missed my mom so much that he couldn't stand being alone. That's why he started dating right away."

Dash hugged her tightly. "You have such a pure heart."

Iris didn't know about that because she kept hoping karma would meet up with her father sooner rather than later. "Now, I see it wasn't like that at all. He'd been with that woman for at least a year, maybe two, before my mom died. What kind of person does that?"

"A monster." Dash pulled Iris onto his lap, and she didn't fight him. "I hate that he's kept hurting you."

"Finding out the truth was hard, but there's something else." Her throat was scratchy, but she kept breathing and no tears fell. Progress from when Henry gave her the report. "The PI told my father that the state had an unclaimed check with our two names on it. It would take both his signature and mine to claim the money. It wasn't a small amount. My dad said his daughter was dead. His exact words were 'Iris is dead. Just like her mother.'"

The stinging at the corner of her eyes made her blink. She shuddered. No way did she want to cry.

"Hey, I've got you." Dash's voice was gentle as he rubbed her arm. "Just say the word, and I'll destroy him."

She almost laughed. Instead, she cuddled against Dash, grateful he had her back. "He's not worth the effort or the jail time."

"I wouldn't go to jail." The words shot out with a sniper's precision.

Iris hadn't seen him like this before, but she appreciated how quick he was to offer help. "You're that confident in your people?"

"In my computer skills," Dash admitted with a gleam of pride in his eyes. "You can ruin a person without ever touching them physically."

She shivered. "I'm sure you could, but don't. Please."

Dash's jaw jutted forward. "He hurt you."

"Yes, but that's on him." She rested her palm on Dash's chest. The beat of his heart soothed her. "I won't let what he did define me. That's what my mom would tell me to do. I just hope she didn't know about his affair because she loved him so much."

"Your mom was an amazing woman. Your compassion and intelligence came from her." Dash toyed with her ponytail. "If she'd known about your dad, she would have told you. Warned you. She loved you."

"That's what I think, too." Iris hugged him. His scent—so much better than any dessert—tickled her nose. "Thank you."

Iris had no idea how long they sat there, but she didn't care. She longed to regain the closeness she'd once shared with Dash, and they'd far surpassed that tonight.

"You doing okay?" he asked finally.

"Yes, I needed this, but I must be getting heavy." She went to move off him.

He tightened his arms around her. "You're not."

She snuggled against his neck. "Good, because this is nice."

"It is." He sounded as if he were smiling.

This was not where she'd expected to find herself tonight, but she had no regrets. "I wish…"

"What?"

She lifted her head to look at him. His blue-eyed gaze focused on her. The affection she saw in their depths gave her the courage to continue. "That we could always be this close. Not just physically…"

The easy smile on his face made her heart beat double time. "I'd like that, too."

A longing she'd buried deep years ago rushed to

the surface. Dash had been there when her mom died and after her dad left. He'd made mistakes, but he'd given her so much when she had nothing, not even a place to stay.

But here, now, she wanted more.

If she was being honest with herself, she'd always wanted more.

This, however, was as close as she'd been to getting what she wanted.

Dare I ask? If she didn't, she might regret it the way she had the last time. A battle raged in her head, but she would follow her heart. "There's something else I wish for."

"I'll give you whatever you want." He sounded so serious. "Just tell me what it is."

Her palms sweated. *Here goes nothing.* "A kiss."

Desire flickered in his gaze. "Are you asking or telling me?"

She wet her lips. "Both?"

"You just shared something emotional. I don't want to take advantage of the situation."

"You're not." Her body tingled with anticipation. "Promise."

A charming smile spread across his handsome face. The color of his eyes deepened to a sapphire blue. "Now?"

Not trusting her voice, she nodded.

As Dash lowered his mouth to hers, Iris met him halfway. His lips touched hers, not accidentally this time, but with a tenderness that made her feel cherished and adored. For so long, Dash had provided her a place to live, but in this moment, she'd found home, the place she belonged and wanted to stay…forever.

Nothing else mattered, but being in his arms with her lips against his…

His kiss was warm, and his taste, a mixture of salt, beer, and Dash, consumed Iris, lighting a flame inside her.

She increased the pressure of their kiss, wrapping her arms around him so she could be even closer to him. His hands were in her hair and on her back.

It was just her and Dash, and she wouldn't want it any other way. No one had ever kissed her so thoroughly with a grand finale of fireworks exploding with each touch of his lips.

One question hammered in her brain.

Why had they waited so long to do this?

Because kissing him was as close to heaven on earth as she'd been, and she didn't want the feeling to end.

Chapter Thirteen

Why had they waited so long to do this?

As they kissed, Dash soaked in the taste of Iris. Not even the beer masked her sweetness. It was better than any dessert she'd made for him and his new favorite flavor that could easily turn into an addiction of the best kind. One he wouldn't mind.

He moved his lips over hers.

Soft.

Holding her, kissing her, was overdue. He enjoyed the peck the other night, but he was loving this slow, hot kiss. Nothing had ever felt so right, no kiss as satisfying, and he wanted to keep touching and tasting her for as long as he could.

Mine.

I want her to be mine.

He remembered their almost-kiss years ago. For someone so smart, he'd made a terrible decision when they were younger because they could have spent all this time kissing.

How perfect would that have been?

Dash tightened his hold on her as if they could stay like this forever.

Forever friends.

His neck prickled. Something that had nothing to do with Iris's lips against his. He lowered his hands and slowly backed away from the kiss, even though he wanted to continue.

She was flushed and breathless. Her pupils were dilated.

His heart stuttered. His pulse revved faster.

He'd never seen her look so gorgeous.

Dash touched her cheek, softly, tentatively, wanting to memorize every part of her face. He also needed to remind himself he wasn't dreaming. This was real, and her lips belonged against his. But before he could kiss her again—he really wanted to do that—they needed to talk. To make sure they both understood what was happening.

Beyond the kissing.

Because their friendship was the most important—most valuable—thing to him. "Hey."

As Iris stared up through her eyelashes, she moistened her lips.

It was all Dash could do not to kiss her again.

Focus, Cabot. "Thanks."

The word was inadequate. It was all he could say because "Stay with me for the rest of eternity" didn't seem appropriate.

"You're welcome?" She sounded unsure.

I feel the same way.

Dash started to speak and then stopped himself. Kissing her again would be so much easier than talking. He lowered his hand. "This is harder than I thought it would be."

She half laughed. "I suppose after a toe-curling kiss we should expect a little awkwardness."

His breath hitched. "Your toes curled?"

She nodded. "Didn't yours?"

Heat rushed up his neck. "To be honest, I wasn't paying attention to my feet."

And his temperature still hadn't settled. Nor his pulse. His breathing was off, too.

She met his gaze. "I'll take that as a compliment."

He tried not to stare at her full, lush lips. Tried and failed. "It's meant to be one."

"I'd better move." She scooted off his lap, and he instantly missed her warmth. "Your legs must be numb."

"Not quite." A good thing she wasn't too far away or he'd be moving closer to her. "But if they were, it would be worth it. I enjoy kissing you."

"Same." She smiled softly. "I could get used to it."

"Me, too." It might be too soon to admit he was there. That reminded him of the reason he'd stopped kissing. "Except how does kissing work with us being friends?"

"You put your lips against mine." Amusement gleamed in her gaze. "Or I put mine against yours."

"Ha-ha. It's just..." His knee bounced. Dash placed his hand on top of it. Around her, he was like a livewire full of nervous energy and attraction. "I don't want anything to ruin our friendship."

Her forehead creased, turning her expression into a worried one. "You think our kissing might?"

"I have no idea, but I want to make sure it won't." Dash kept his voice steady, but his concerns didn't make that easy. "I screwed things up once. Now, we're still trying to get our friendship back on track. Add in my breaking it off with Raina and you starting culinary school, a relationship..."

"Whoa." She touched the side of his head. "Stop thinking so hard."

"What?" he asked, confused.

"We've had one—well, let's call it one and a half kisses, and your brilliant brain is moving at light speed." She lowered her arm and then smiled. "Slow down, okay?"

He had been thinking in terms of eternity, so maybe she had a valid point. "What do you suggest?"

"Your entire body tensed when you said relationship, so forget labels."

"No friends-with-kissing-benefits, then?" he joked, trying to lighten the mood.

She groaned. "Please, no. But we can focus on being better friends and becoming closer."

Did having her sit on his lap count as close? Probably better if he didn't ask that.

"Things will never be how they used to be. We're not the same people we were then," she continued. "It's up to us to define what friendship means for us now."

"Like if we kiss?"

Iris nodded. "The entire time we've known each other, all I've wanted is to make things easier on you. This is no different. As long as we promise to protect our friendship, no matter what, this should work."

She'd done that for him over the years, especially since he hired her, but what she said raised a question he needed to ask. This shouldn't be all about him. "Is this what you want?"

A wistful expression crossed her face. "I'm okay with it for now."

For now. Not forever.

Okay, Dash understood. She wanted the fairy-tale ending. Something he didn't believe in. "You want more someday."

Iris nodded. "Emphasis on someday. I can wait."

Wait for him? Or someone else?

Dash didn't want to know the answer, but *for now* was better than the alternative—nothing. "So our friendship comes first."

"Yes, but…" She bit her lip. "Being friends has to be a priority."

"It is," he blurted, not wanting her to doubt him. "I've learned my lesson."

"I didn't mean you." Iris held his hand. "I said that aloud to remind myself with classes starting."

"Neither of us will forget." Dash wanted to reassure her. He squeezed her hand. "I promise I won't."

"I promise, too." Iris moved closer until she was almost on his lap again. "Want to seal this deal with a kiss?"

Dash answered by pressing his lips against hers. She met his kiss with an eagerness of her own, putting her hands in his hair before he could get his arms around her. The blood in his veins heated, not that it had cooled much.

This kiss was better than the last one. He couldn't wait to see if the trend continued. Kissing Iris was now his new favorite pastime.

* * *

On Monday morning, Dash sat at his desk, reviewing a quality report from an engineer about the new prototype. A text notification sounded. He glanced at his cell phone's screen, and warmth flowed through him.

THE DEAL BREAKER

The selfie of Iris wearing her culinary school uniform—a pair of black pants and a white coat with embroidery on the left side above a pocket was like a ray of sunshine breaking through this wet, winter day. Her hair was pulled off her face, and she wore a white cap. Her happy smile told him that she was where she needed to be.

Even though he'd fought it, he agreed and supported her. She deserved the opportunity to finish what she'd started ten years ago. Smiling, he read her message.

Iris: *Took me forever to remember how to tie the neckerchief, and you can't even see it. At least I look like a chef. First step to becoming one.*
Dash: *You look great.*
Iris: *Only eighteen months to go. LOL!*
Dash: *It'll go by fast.*
Iris: *Break over. TTYL.*

Texts didn't convey emotion, but Dash sensed her excitement. The feeling was contagious because this meant so much to her. He wanted to do something special for Iris to celebrate her first day. Those were the hardest and most tiring since it was something new. She had classes early tomorrow, so going out wouldn't work, but a meal at home with a special dessert and a foot rub might be nice.

He texted Tony.

Dash: *Any chance you can make a dessert to celebrate Iris's first day.*
Cook: *I'll get on it. She's still a chocoholic, right?*
Dash: *Yes.*
Cook: *It'll pair nicely with tonight's menu. Thanks.*

No, thank you. He should change the "Cook" to "Chef" or "Tony," but part of him hadn't been sure the guy would last. Especially the way he'd flirted with Iris. That didn't worry Dash now.

Hours later, he found himself in the middle of a project about to implode. He checked the time. No way would he be home for dinner, which bummed him out. Dash had been thinking about seeing Iris all day, but he needed to be here. He typed a text.

Dash: *Have to work late. Fire needs extinguishing.*
Iris: *Good luck!*
Dash: *Tony's making you something special.*
Iris: *So that's what smells delicious.*
Dash: *My idea, so I deserve full credit unless it's bad.*
Iris: *Ha-ha. I'll save you some.*
Dash: *See you later.*

Unfortunately, issues with the project continued. Dash missed Iris.

Dash: *How was dinner?*
Iris: *Delicious. Janice, Leo, and Tony ate with me.*

Iris: *Oh, and I'll send a pic of the yummy dessert.*
Dash: *Can't wait to see it or you. I have more work to do. May sleep here.*
Iris: *Take care.*
Dash: *Don't eat my slice.*
Iris: *I'd never do that.*
Dash: *Never say never. Sweet dreams.*
Iris: *Hope everything gets fixed.*

He ended up sleeping on the futon in his office. Something he'd done many times before, but he wanted to be at home tonight. Not seeing Iris bugged him.

The next day, much to his frustration, the project was still off the rails. Dash did what he could to help the stressed-out team leader. He'd created the algorithms. No one knew them better, including the company's Chief Technical Officer. The only good parts of his day were the texts from Iris. Not that he had time to reply.

That night, a bag containing a milkshake, cheeseburger, fries, and a cookie was delivered to his office from his favorite fast food place. She'd texted him earlier saying a surprise was on the way, so he knew this was from Iris.

His heart overflowed with warmth. Dash only wished he could see her. That reminded him. He still hadn't answered her texts, so he sent two messages. One to thank her. The other a selfie. She replied with a photo of herself giving him the thumbs-up sign. Cute, but he would rather be in the pic with her.

Did they have any photos of them together?

He didn't think so. A quick scroll through his photos confirmed that. They would need to remedy that when he was home tomorrow.

At lunchtime the next day, Dash went home to change clothes, but Iris was at school. He couldn't say they were two ships passing in the night because until today they hadn't been close enough to do that.

Standing in front of her bedroom door, he used his phone to take a picture. He texted it to her and wrote "wish you were here."

Iris: *Will I see you tonight?*
Dash: *I'm trying to get out of a business dinner.*
Iris: *Work is important.*
Dash: *So are you.*
Iris: *Awww.*
Dash: *I miss you.*
Iris: *Same. If you have to go, I'll wait up.*
Dash: *I'd love that. Thanks.*

He appreciated Iris's understanding. His frustration, however, kept building. Not seeing her these past three days was driving him crazy. She was *always* on his mind. He'd never felt that way before about anyone, and he wasn't sure what to make of it. Maybe he missed her so much because things were so new between them. Whatever the reason, he hoped to be with her soon.

Dash asked if his dinner scheduled for tonight with a potential customer, a CEO and her staff, could be postponed or if he could skip it. But his assistant, Fallon, and a VP told him he couldn't unless a snowstorm shut down Portland. Unfortunately, the forecast predicted rain and temperatures in the forties when he needed a Snowmageddon.

If only...

Being stuck with Iris would be the perfect way to spend a snow day. They'd hung out together whenever school was canceled when they were younger, either playing video games or watching a movie marathon or a combination of both. She would grab food for them downstairs in her parents' restaurant.

Speaking of the forecast...

Cloud seeding had been used for rain and rockets to attract lightning, but maybe he should ask the lab to look into the latest research on weather manipulation because he'd thought about this before. Might come in handy.

At dinner, Dash's VP did most of the talking, leaving him to answer specific questions. The restaurant had stellar reviews from food critics who had deemed it the place to eat. He didn't understand why. Fancy cocktails aside, the tiny appetizers covering the table wouldn't satisfy a hungry hamster.

He doubted the entrees would be more filling.

He forced himself to pay attention to what the others were saying. It wasn't easy. Despite what the contract would be worth to his company, he wanted to be home. Strike that, he didn't care where he was as long as Iris was with him.

A little after ten o'clock, Dash arrived home. He yawned. All he wanted to do was see Iris and then sleep. Talk about tired.

Someone was talking, but he didn't recognize the voice. As he went into the great room, he saw a cooking show on the TV.

Dash didn't see anyone, but then he noticed Iris asleep on the couch. A gray cashmere throw covered her.

Even if he'd wanted to tumble into his bed thirty seconds ago, seeing her energized him. As he moved closer, his fingers itched to run through her hair or touch her. He did neither.

Instead, he watched her.

Given Iris's smile, her dream must be a good one. So pretty.

She used her bent arm as a pillow. Her sock-covered feet stuck out from the blanket. She looked so comfortable. If there'd been room for him, he would have joined her.

But there wasn't. That left him one question to answer—let Iris sleep or wake her?

Dash wanted her to remain in dreamland, but he

had no idea if she'd set an alarm for the morning. Being on time was important to her. Always had been, even when they were in high school. Iris had mentioned her schedule to him. She liked arriving early at the culinary school so she could change and be in her first class on time. That was when she sent him her first text of the day.

Waking her was the right choice.

He kneeled next to the sofa. "Hey, Sleeping Beauty."

She didn't stir. Maybe his voice was too soft. He would try again.

"Iris," he said louder before touching her shoulder. "Come on, gorgeous. It's time to go to bed."

She blinked open her eyes, and she turned her head to look up at him. "What?"

He brushed back the hair that had fallen onto her face. "You fell asleep watching television."

"I was waiting up for you." She sounded tired.

Dash kissed her forehead. "I'm sorry I was so late."

"No apology necessary." Iris stretched. "Did you get the contract?"

"It looks like we will."

"Yay."

He smiled, more happy to be home with her than what profit his company would make with the new customer. "At least my time was well-spent, even if I thought about you all night."

"Funny, because you were on my mind, too."

"I was?" He feigned shock. That was better than grinning like a fool. "What were you thinking?"

Her lower lip stuck out. "I was going to ask that."

"You answer, then I will."

"Sounds fair." She rose up on her elbow. "I was thinking how nice getting a hug and a kiss would be."

"That's funny, because I thought the same thing."

She grinned. "GMTA."

Great minds think alike. True, and he had another acronym for her. "LWMK."

Her eyebrows drew together. "I don't know that one."

"Lips want more kisses."

Iris's face scrunched. "You made that up."

He shrugged. "Yeah. The real meaning is locking wall mount kit, but I prefer my definition."

Especially with Iris.

She nodded. "So do I."

That was the only invitation Dash needed. He leaned closer, touching his mouth to hers. She tasted like peppermint, but the same underlying Iris—sweetness—was also there.

He'd missed this.

Missed her.

Dash kept the kiss light because they didn't need to rush into anything.

Iris backed away first. "We need a new rule."

"You're thinking of rules during a hot kiss?"

"It was hot, but that's why." Laughter lit her eyes. "The new rule should be whenever one of us comes home, we have to greet the other with a kiss like that."

"Oh, good one. And I second it." He also enjoyed hearing her call this place "home." It was for now, and maybe, if things kept going well, it would be her home in the future.

Chapter Fourteen

As Iris finished the second week of culinary school, she'd never been happier. Glancing in the mirror, she removed the rubber band from her ponytail and shook out her hair. She changed into a pair of leggings and a large sweatshirt, perfect Friday night clothing.

Dash had canceled their plans on Tuesday when Mason asked for help with something. Tonight was Dash's way of making that up to her—pizza and video games. He'd given her the choice of what to play. She chose Mario Kart because she could beat him at that.

Not that Iris needed to win. She would leave that to Blaise Mortenson. Being with Dash was the best prize ever. This past week, she wondered if her feet even touched the ground. Tony asked if she would sign a prenup. Leo told her she had a bounce to her step. Janice mentioned Iris's glowing complexion.

Iris just smiled, but she knew things were going well. She enjoyed her classes, and spending time with Dash was wonderful. For a guy who didn't know the definition of romance, he was doing a good job being romantic. Whenever they were together, he focused solely on her.

No pulling out his cell phone. No distractions.

Mr. Status Quo appeared to be embracing the changes with her and their friendship so well that he might need a new nickname.

That brought a smile.

She headed downstairs to see if Tony needed help with dinner.

So far, she and Dash had eaten out, visited an arcade, and gone bowling. At home, they'd binge watched series and caught up on movies neither had seen. No matter what they did or even when they did nothing but talk, each minute was better than the next

Their friendship was growing stronger. No, it wasn't the same as it had been, but there was a bonus.

The kisses...

Those were the cherries on top of a decadent hot fudge sundae with scoops of her favorite ice cream and freshly made whipped cream. Only, the kisses had no calories so she could splurge often.

And did.

Iris went into the kitchen to find Tony standing at the island. He appeared to have everything under control. He'd even filled bowls with candy, nuts, and chips. But the pizzas on the counter...

She eyed each one, cataloging the ingredients. Pesto sauce, mozzarella cheese, sundried tomatoes, artichoke hearts, and pine nuts. Italian sausage and pepperoni. Barbeque chicken with mozzarella, gouda, and red onion. "Wow, those pizzas look amazing."

He flashed a lop-sided smile and added a few more pine nuts. "Wait until you taste them."

She studied the one closest to her. "I'm sure, but that's a lot for two of us."

"Use the leftovers for your lunch tomorrow. These are better than anything you can buy."

She wriggled her toes in anticipation of her move. "Great idea."

Tony brushed his palms together. "I'll see you around, but I want to say thanks again for this job. I love it, and two of Dash's friends have booked me for weekend parties."

"That's wonderful." Iris had finally decided to go to the Super Bowl party on Sunday, but she didn't ask Tony about it in case he wasn't doing that one. She snagged a piece of cheese.

He covered each pizza with plastic wrap. "I'll stick these in the fridge. You know what to do with them."

"Yes, but after this weekend, leave detailed

instructions for Dash, since I won't be here."

"I remember. I've read through your binder twice." Tony laughed. "But I have a feeling you'll be back under this roof sooner rather than later."

Leaving was bittersweet. Iris liked the three people she'd hired. Most of all, she enjoyed staying at Dash's house and seeing him so much, but she couldn't deny her excitement of moving into her own apartment. "True, we'll hang out here more."

Tony shook his head. "That's not what I meant."

Realization dawned. Her face heated. "I signed a year lease."

"So? You're dating a billionaire."

Dating.

The word echoed through her. Iris had yet to describe what she and Dash were doing. Only one person had asked—Janice. Iris had said they were hanging out. That seemed an honest assessment, even if her affection kept deepening. Not using labels had been her idea to keep Dash from stressing out. But she couldn't deny Tony saying they were dating sent a thrill shooting through her.

"You never know," Iris said finally.

Tony winked. "I signed an NDA so you're safe if you want to spill."

She laughed. "When there's something to tell, I will."

The status quo was fine right now.

"I'm holding you to that." Tony washed and dried

his hands. "Happy moving day. Enjoy the new place."

"Have a great weekend."

As he left, Iris carried the snack bowls to the great room and then brought out the gaming chairs. Dash had a special room set up where he usually played, but she didn't game intensely as he did. Using the system down here would be better.

Her cell phone buzzed. She read the text.

Dash: *Leaving now.*
Iris: *See you soon.*

She preheated the ovens. Two pizzas would fit in the larger one.

By the time Iris had trivets, plates, and napkins in the great room, the timer beeped. She placed the pizzas in the ovens and reset the timer. Dinner would be ready when Dash walked in the door.

It was almost like playing house.

Emphasis on playing.

Iris laughed because her life had never been like the families she'd seen on television. She ate her meals at a corner table by herself until she was old enough to carry a plate upstairs to their apartment or help out downstairs. Both her parents cooked in the restaurant. Her mother also helped in the front of the house when the hostess or servers needed backup.

"Something smells delicious." Dash entered the kitchen and kissed her. Hard.

THE DEAL BREAKER

When he pulled away, she was breathless. "You're taking the rule seriously."

He smirked. The expression was more sexy than it was annoying. "Go big or go home."

She hugged him. "Tony made three pizzas, and I've set out everything."

Something flashed in Dash's eyes, but whatever it was disappeared in an instant. "Oh, right. I have until nine. Though I need to pack."

Wait. What? She stepped back. "Where are you going?"

"Florida."

"Tonight?"

He grabbed two beers out of the refrigerator and opened them. "Blaise scored Super Bowl tickets for us, so we're doing an impromptu bachelor party for Wes and going to the game. It'll be epic."

Epic. Maybe for him. She thought about moving into her apartment tomorrow and the party he'd asked her to attend. "So no Super Bowl party."

It wasn't a question. "Canceled, but you said you weren't sure you wanted to go."

"I decided to go with you." After she'd turned down another invitation from a classmate. Guess this was the whirlwind life of a billionaire.

Okay, she was whining. But she'd wanted to share the excitement of her new apartment and spend time with him on Sunday. Now… "I guess it's not every day you get to attend a Super Bowl."

"I've been to a few, but not with everyone." He sipped his beer. "Henry offered up the use of his plane. That's why I need to leave at nine."

Henry had offered Frank's services on her moving day. He'd called to confirm two days ago, but Iris had assumed Dash would help her, so she told Henry no, thanks. Now, she was on her own. At least she could use the dolly in the garage.

Dash squeezed her shoulder. "Hey, you're okay with this, right?"

"It's…sudden."

He laughed. "That happens with us. Hadley, who is OCD about planning, gets annoyed sometimes."

Iris knew how the matchmaker felt. "It's just… Tonight's my last night here. I move into my apartment tomorrow."

His mouth dropped open. He scrubbed his face before reaching out and placing his hands on her shoulders. "I forgot."

His words hit hard.

Her lungs constricted, making it hard to breathe. Iris felt as if being forgotten at Christmastime was happening all over again. She stared at the wood floor.

"I'm sorry." His apology flew out. "Having you here has been so perfect, I didn't want to think about you leaving. When the guys talked about a bachelor party and Super Bowl game, everything else went out of my mind."

Including her.

A part of her understood. A trip with his closest guy friends would be fun. They fed off each other and could be guilty of tunnel vision when something interested them. But another part hated the hurtful memories being dredged up.

He raised her chin with his finger. "I'm so sorry."

"Moving into an apartment doesn't compare to your plans, but I wish you'd have at least remembered."

Tomorrow was an important day for her. One she'd wanted to share with him.

"Hey." His gaze zeroed in on her. "I know how excited you are about having your own place. I made a mistake. Forgive me, please."

Dash sounded sincere, and the regret in his eyes was unmistakable.

"I forgive you." She forced her shoulders back. "A bachelor party and the Super Bowl are big deals."

"So is your first apartment." His eyebrows wrinkled. "This coming week is busy, but I'll make it up to you on Thursday. We'll do something extra-special."

Her birthday was Thursday. Earlier this month, Dash promised to make up for not getting her a Christmas present. Guess that meant he would go all-out. She wiggled her toes. "I'd love that."

"It's a date." A charming smile lit up his face. "On Friday night, let's go to Hood Hamlet for the weekend. Henry and Wes have places there. I'll ask if one is free, and if not, find another place. Sound good?"

Celebrating her birthday for four days would not only be fun but also a first. "I'd love that."

The timer dinged.

"Pizza's ready." She put on an oven mitt, removed the pizzas one by one, and sliced them. "I can carry them to the table."

"I've got the beer."

She nodded.

"But first"—Dash wrapped his hands around hers—"I know things have come up with my mom, my dad, Mason, and now the guys to keep us apart. But you are the most important person in my life. When we finish eating, I'll prove it to you with make up kisses."

"Make up kisses?"

"Trust me." He kissed her forehead. "Nothing matters more than you, okay?"

Her throat thickened. She wanted to believe him. She really did.

* * *

After dinner and a few rounds of Mario Kart, Iris packed Dash's clothes for his trip while he sat on his bed watching her. If she let him do this, he'd take sweats, shorts, and T-shirts, and she'd be getting a call from a VP at his company if a photograph showed him dressed that way.

Packing and laying out what he wore was no longer her job, but Janice and Leo had plans to go out to dinner. Iris didn't want to disturb them. Plus, this gave her more time with Dash.

Her evening had turned out better than she expected given the start. He was sorry, and she would only drive herself crazy dwelling on it, so they'd put what happened behind them and moved on. Winning each race had helped. So did the delicious pizza and Dash's make up kisses. Knowing he had something special in store for Thursday didn't hurt. She had a feeling this would be her best birthday ever.

Dash watched her. "I don't know how you beat me every time."

Iris tucked the shirt in her hand under her arm and wiggled her fingers. "Mad skills."

"I've practiced."

"I'm the master. You're the apprentice," she teased, adding another shirt into his bag.

He peered inside the suitcase. "We're flying home after the game on Sunday. I don't need that many clothes."

"I texted Henry to get an idea of the itinerary."

"He's a clotheshorse."

"Henry is stylish, and you shouldn't wear something that's dirty and smells."

"I—"

She shot him a hard look. "Remember when you

came home for spring break your freshman year of college?"

He'd only brought clothes that fit into his backpack, so he could carry his various gaming consoles in his roll-on suitcase. His mother nearly passed out when she'd done his laundry.

A sheepish expression crossed his face. "I was eighteen."

"Old enough to know better."

"I've stopped doing that."

She placed her hands on her hips. "Excuse me? You've stopped?"

He winked. "You make sure I don't end up on the Board's naughty list."

"That's part of my job." Or was. Dressing him was Leo's responsibility now.

When Dash was in his early twenties, Maya Ruiz had been hired to be VP of customer service and, unofficially, Dash's handler. She helped him to adjust to running a multi-billion-dollar company and kept the young founder, with Iris's help, from showing up to shareholder events or media interviews in a stained hoodie, holey sweats, and ripped Chucks.

"You're old enough to know how to dress. You just take the easy way out by having someone pick out your clothes for you."

"It's a billionaire perk," he said nonchalantly. "But I still won't wear half of what you're packing."

"You'll have them if you need them." She'd done

her job.

For the last time.

Iris brushed off the twinge of sadness. He was in good hands.

His black travel kit went in next. It contained smaller portions of what he used at home and remained packed for his trips. "That's the final item."

Admiration glinted in his eyes. "You've got this down to a science."

She zipped the suitcase and then set it on the carpet. "I've practiced."

He laughed. "I'll miss you."

Iris wished he didn't have to go. "You'll be back soon."

"I'm not talking about this trip." His gaze grew serious. "If you don't like living in the apartment, for whatever reason, you have a place here."

Her breath caught in her throat. "Thanks. I hope I love it, but I appreciate having a backup plan."

"Sit."

She sat next to him on the bed.

"I have something for you." Dash wiped his hands on his pants before leaning over and pulling a piece of paper off his nightstand. "I need you to fill out the information that's marked with the flag."

Iris took the document and unfolded it. She gasped. "It's a car title."

"I'm making you a joint owner on the Range Rover. You won't have to worry about insurance or maintenance. Just gas. Unless you want a gas card."

"No, thanks." A part of her loved having access to the car. That would help when she had her externship at a local restaurant or café in Portland to gain professional experience, but... "I appreciate the offer, but I don't want to be someone you *have* to give things to."

"You are nothing like my mother and father. You've never asked me for anything. That's why I want to do this for you. Plus, I'm being selfish."

She tilted her head, trying to figure out what he meant. "Selfish?"

"How will you get here from your apartment?"

Iris hadn't thought she'd go to his house once she left. All she'd considered was the location in relation to the culinary school, so she could walk. "I haven't figured that out yet."

"You mentioned having a budget," he said without missing a beat. "Ride services add up. There isn't a bus stop within walking distance, either. I can pick you up and drop you off, but that could make things difficult with my schedule. If you had a car, that's one less thing I have to do."

Dash had a point. "I hadn't thought of that."

Straightening, he grinned with pride. "I finally thought of something before you."

That surprised her, but it also pleased her at the same time. Dash was changing and in good ways. Still... She glanced at the title and then at him. "This feels like too much."

"It's not." He placed his arm around her. "But if you won't do it for yourself, please do it for me. I won't worry as much knowing you have safe, reliable transportation. See, selfish."

That made her laugh.

He pulled her to his side. "Is that a yes?"

Iris blew out a breath. The car meant nothing to him. He'd only bought it so she'd have something to drive to the grocery store and to run his errands. "You really want…"

"I really do."

"O-kay, but if you need it back, just say the word."

"I won't," he said a beat later. "After you fill the title out, leave it on my nightstand."

"Thank you."

"No, thank you." He kissed her quick on the lips. "This is as much for me as for you."

She eyed him with suspicion. "Or might this be another billionaire perk?"

His expression turned mischievous. "Perhaps it's both. Is that so bad that I want you to have everything you need?"

Dash was sweet. "No, I feel the same about you, but I don't give you expensive gifts."

"You would if you could," he said with certainty.

"Maybe." No, that wasn't true. "Probably."

He kissed her forehead. "Thanks for admitting

that. I need to get downstairs. Henry—well, Frank—is picking me up."

Dash held out his hand, and Iris grabbed it. Their fingers laced. "I'm so lucky to have you as my friend."

"Soon to be your best friend," he corrected.

"It'll happen." The way they spent time together and communicated, Iris had a feeling it wouldn't be long until they were best friends again.

And maybe…more.

Chapter Fifteen

Sunday night, Dash sat in the cabin of Henry's plane. The lights were dimmed. Someone snored. Most likely Wes, who'd enjoyed his bachelor weekend, letting loose for the first time since his remission. Before kickoff, however, Wes had claimed never to take another shot again. No one believed him, but all promised not to mention how much he'd drunk on Saturday.

Dash stared at his tablet. Still no texts from Iris. He'd received a few photos from her apartment, but nothing last night or today. He'd sent her pics from the game, but she hadn't replied. That wasn't like her.

He hoped everything was okay.

If it weren't…

Adrenaline shot through him.

Iris had just moved in. She hadn't been there long enough to meet her neighbors. If she fell or got sick, no one would know because she lived alone. He shifted in the leather captain's seat.

There was Wi-Fi on the plane. He might as well use it.

Dash: *Flying back. How's the apartment?*

Delivered was beneath the reply. But no dots appeared to tell him she was typing.
He waited.
Nothing.

Dash: *Did you watch the game?*

Again, he waited.
Same result.
No reply.
His knee bounced.
Where could she be?

Dash: *Haven't heard from you today. Please check in.*

He scanned his inbox and opened an email from one of his executive team, but as he read, his irritation at not hearing from Iris grew. So did his worry.

This would drive him crazy. Who was he kidding? It already was.

Dash blew out his breath, and even though his phone notified him of incoming texts, he double-checked to see if any had arrived.

None had.

"What's wrong, Wonderkid?" Mason asked from across the aisle. "Only make two billion last quarter instead of four?"

Man, Dash was thirsty. He reached for his water bottle and gulped. "Why do you think something's wrong?"

"Subtlety isn't your superpower, dude."

No, it wasn't.

Mason leaned toward him. "Tell me what's going on."

"I can't reach Iris," Dash admitted, feeling useless and helpless. Not a good combination. "I keep thinking something might have happened to her."

"I thought she quit."

"She did."

Mason scratched the scruff on his chin. "So why are you worried about her?"

Dash would have laughed at Mason's puzzled expression if he wasn't so concerned about Iris. But he couldn't miss the opportunity to get back at the founder of the fastest growing social media platform. "Looks like observation skills aren't your superpower."

"Wait." Lines creased Mason's forehead. "You and Iris?"

Dash nodded.

"No wonder you were so upset she was leaving." Mason grinned. "All I can say is it's about time."

"What do you mean?" Dash asked.

"She's been a surrogate wife for as long as I've known you. I love Rachael, but she doesn't do all the things Iris does for you."

"It's her job. She has a strong work ethic."

"She does, but for you, she doesn't go above and beyond. It's more like, in the immortal words of Buzz Lightyear, Iris goes to infinity and beyond."

Everything she did appeared to be so effortless. "I took her for granted."

"Yep, the two of you were practically married," Mason joked. "Might as well make it official."

"Not funny."

Mason's mouth fell open. "You're totally gone for her."

"We're friends. I…" Dash glanced at his phone. Still no reply. A hundred and three scenarios ran through his head. None good. His chest tightened. "Yeah, I am."

Mason's face brightened. "So when are you going to put a ring on it?"

Henry leaned around in his seat. "Did someone mention a ring?"

Mason nodded, grinning like a fool. "Dash is crazy about Iris."

"About time." Henry smirked.

Mason laughed. "That's what I said. Now if Wes and Paige have a spring wedding, and then Dash proposes and marries Iris before July thirteenth, the bet is off and we split the fund."

Dash shook his head. "Should have known the bet's all you cared about."

"It's not the only thing." Mason motioned to Dash's phone. "Still, no word?"

Nothing was on his screen. He slumped. "Nope."

Henry's gaze darkened. "Is something wrong?"

"Iris hasn't replied to any texts, and Wonderkid is worried about her," Mason explained.

"Thank you for that recap, Mase." Henry appeared to be holding in a laugh. He looked at Dash. "Want me to see what I can find out?"

Dash straightened. "Yes, please. Iris mentioned you hired her a PI."

"I don't need him for this." Henry grinned sheepishly. "I know the manager of the apartment building where Iris lives. I'll have her check on her newest tenant."

Huh? Something didn't sound right. Especially knowing how easily Iris had found her place after having so much trouble.

Dash narrowed his gaze. "How do you know the manager?"

"I just do."

"Not good enough," Dash pressed. "Explain what's going on."

"Nothing really."

Dash raised a brow.

"Okay," Henry relented. "I bought the building. It's not officially mine until the deal closes, but the manager has been a big help."

"I told Dash to buy her a condo, but you bought the entire building," Mason gushed. "Sweet."

Dash's mouth went dry. "Why?"

Henry raised his chin. "Because none of the places on her list were good enough for her. I had my doubts if you would step up, so I took matters into my own hands."

Dash's heart pounded in his ears. "I only found out that Friday night."

As he spoke, the words sounded like an excuse. Which they were. All he'd done was say he could buy a place. Henry hadn't asked or offered, he'd taken action and done it.

"There wasn't much time before she ended up in an undesirable place. She's intent on sticking to her budget and making her money last. So I did the only thing I could think of." He didn't sound the least bit apologetic. "I bought the building on Saturday while Iris was in the ladies' room. I had the manager pay a tenant to give up his lease so Iris could move in."

Mason high-fived Henry. "That's master level right there."

"It is." Dash felt hot all over. He rubbed his forehead. "I appreciate what you did for Iris, but I need to know she's okay. Could you text the property manager?"

"I'll do it right now." Henry sat forward.

Mason patted Dash's shoulder. "She's probably busy unpacking. Moving is a lot of work."

Especially when she was likely doing it on her own. At the front of the cabin, Frank sat next to Lex and Rico, Dash's security team, and Craig, who worked for Wes. Not that Iris had a ton of stuff.

The amount didn't matter.
It was still moving.

"What you're feeling sucks," Mason said, showing uncharacteristic empathy. "Rachael and I had been dating a few weeks when she drove to Salem to visit a friend. I couldn't reach her for hours. I was sure she had wrecked on I-5 or been kidnapped. But she was having fun and hadn't realized her phone was off."

Dash hoped Iris's cell phone was the issue, not her. "At least nothing was wrong with Rachael."

"Yeah, but the hours until I heard from her were the worst. I even went to her apartment. I felt like a total stalker, but I'd never experienced such all-consuming worry. That's when I knew."

"Knew what?"

"That she was the one." Mason smiled. "My app lets me follow where she is, but that's why I wanted her—us—to be the first to try your tracker prototype. I can't imagine anything happening to her. She's my life."

Could Dash say the same thing about Iris?

He didn't know.

But she was more than just a friend. He could admit that now. "I'm happy you found Rachael."

"Me, too." Mason got a faraway look in his eyes. "You're Mr. Status Quo, but falling for the right woman is worth mixing things up. She's changed my world and my outlook. I'm a better person because of her."

"More so when you're physically with Rachael," Henry quipped. "But she is good for you. As is Cambria for Adam, Selah for Kieran, Hadley for Blaise, Paige for Wes, and Iris for Master Dashiell, here."

"Did you reach the manager?" Dash asked, digging his fingers into his seat.

"I did." Henry smiled at him. "Iris's phone is dead. She can't find her charger, so she may have left it at your house."

Dash released the breath he'd been holding. "Why didn't she buy another one?"

"Because Iris has one and wants to stick to her budget," Henry explained. "If you're that upset about it, find Iris's and take it to her."

Dash's jaw jutted forward. "I'll do that."

Henry sighed. "But please not tonight. She has class in the morning. And you've barely slept."

"Fine." But first thing tomorrow, Dash would be at Iris's door with a phone charger. Either hers, or one of his.

THE DEAL BREAKER

* * *

So much for being at Iris's door first thing. Henry hadn't mentioned the building's security system, but knowing strangers couldn't walk in off the street pleased Dash. That made up for him standing in the dark outside the building. His breath hung in the air. At least he'd worn gloves, thanks to Leo.

Iris's name wasn't on the listing, but Henry had told Dash the address and unit number. He shifted the bag of doughnuts into his left hand and then glanced at his phone.

6:18 AM.

She was always up this early at his house.

Dash hit the button for her apartment.

"Hello?" She sounded tentative. At this hour, he didn't blame her.

"It's me. Dash," he said into the speaker. "You forgot your phone charger. I brought it to you."

"Oh, thanks. I'll let you in."

A second later, the door buzzed. He went inside to the lobby. The air smelled like lemons. The hardwood floor gleamed. Numbered mailboxes lined one wall. Artwork hung above a table on the other. An upholstered chair sat in the corner by a staircase.

Kudos, Davenport.

This was nicer and cleaner than Dash expected.

He climbed the stairs to the second floor, located Iris's apartment, and knocked.

The door opened.

She wore a sweater and a pair of black leggings tucked into suede boots. An outfit he'd seen her wear before, but his pulse kicked up a notch.

"Good morning." Iris motioned him inside. "I figured you'd sleep in today."

Dash held up her charger. "I wanted to return this, drop off doughnuts, and do this."

He pressed his lips against hers. So warm and sweet. His thoughts stilled, and he lost himself in her kiss. Iris returned his enthusiasm until she stepped back. "Did you say doughnuts?"

Laughing, he handed her the bag and then surveyed her apartment. Small, but nice. He didn't see any furniture except a bed in what appeared to be an alcove off to the right. "I like your place."

Iris's smile lit up her face. The result—breathtaking.

"I love everything about it." She pointed to the window. "Except for the view of the building next door. But I'm not one to stand there and ponder the world through a piece of glass, so I'll be fine."

"I missed you." The three words couldn't adequately describe how being with her filled him with joy. "I'm happy you love your apartment, spot to ponder aside, but I missed you. I hate that this week is so busy for me."

"But you're here now." She raised the bag. "Bearing gifts. And we'll see each other on Thursday and spend the weekend together."

"I'll pick you up at six-thirty." Henry had suggested a trendy private dining club as a special place to take Iris. All Dash needed to do was confirm their reservation since tables were hard to get. "And Henry's house in Hood Hamlet is ours for the weekend."

She inhaled sharply. "Can we go sledding?"

Dash laughed. "That's not what I expected, but we can. I'm happy to do whatever you want, including chocolate tasting."

"I can't wait." Iris bounced up on her toes, planted a kiss on his lips, and then lowered herself. She peeked inside the bag. "I need to eat a doughnut before I head to school. Do you want one?"

"No, thanks. I need to get to work." He wished he could stay with her all day, but she had somewhere to go, too. "Enjoy them."

"I will." Her gaze softened. "I… I really appreciate you dropping by this morning."

"I'm glad I could return your cord." He hated saying goodbye. "See you in a couple of days."

Thursday couldn't arrive soon enough.

* * *

Dash sat at his desk. For days, he'd been in this same position or on the futon trying to rest. He'd asked Janice to clear his personal calendar and Fallon to do the same with his work one. Now he couldn't remember what day it was. If he wasn't sleeping here, he arrived in the dark and left after the sun had gone down.

Thankfully, the staff at the lab addressed each problem. Not that their efforts surprised him. He'd handpicked each one for their jobs, and since the research facility was his baby, he'd stayed to offer support and provide input when asked.

A text arrived. He checked his screen.

Mom: *Your father says the beach house is his this weekend, but I'm on the calendar. Talk to him.*
Dash: *I've spoken to him. This is something you have to do yourself.*
Mom: *I can't.*
Dash: *Please try. I have too much going on right now.*
Mom: *So you're blowing off your own mother for work again?*
Dash: *That's not fair, and you know it. My work supports both you and Dad. And I haven't slept this week.*
Mom: *Are you still at the office?*
Dash: *I was getting ready to leave when you texted.*
Mom: *Fine. Blame me. That's what your father did.*
Dash: *No one is blaming you. I just don't want to be put in the middle again.*
Mom: *Get some sleep. I'll call you tomorrow.*

Why did this keep happening? He cradled his head in his hands. Calling his dad might be easier. Or maybe he could hire someone to manage his parents. Dash loved them, but their daily calls and demands were exhausting him.

He yawned, stretching his arms over his head. The lack of sleep was catching up with him. Not even caffeine was working. He glanced at the clock. After six. Time to get out of here and sleep in his own bed.

A knock sounded on his ajar door. Fallon Caples stuck her head in. "Do you have a minute?"

"Come in."

She wore one of her trademark skirts and matching blazer. Today, the color was hot pink. She was thirty-two, a single mom, and Blaise's sister-in-law. Dash appreciated how fast she caught on to things around here. The ends of her blonde hair swayed as she walked.

She tucked a strand of hair behind her ear. "There's someone at the front desk to see you."

Odd. Usually, Fallon would have used the intercom to tell him, not come in person. "Do they have an appointment?"

"No." She adjusted her skirt. "It's Raina."

He must have heard wrong. "Did you say Raina was here?"

Fallon nodded. "Should I send her up?"

Raina came to his office once when they were leaving from here for an event. She'd been all smiles then, not sad as she was the night they broke up. "I was about to leave, but I can stay for a few minutes."

"I'll let the front desk know." Fallon turned and headed out.

Five minutes later, Raina entered his office. She wore black pants, a sweater, and boots. A leather messenger bag hung from her shoulder. Her hair was loose, the way she normally wore it, but her eyes were red and swollen as if she'd been crying.

He stood. "What's going on?"

She took slow, measured steps. "I'm sorry for coming here without talking to you first, but I didn't know where else to go. I got fired today."

"I'm sorry." Dash walked around his desk. "You helped build that company."

Raina shrugged, but her face pinched. "I don't fit their "new" vision. There was other stuff they said, but it's all a blur right now. I never expected this to happen."

He motioned to a chair. As she sat, he leaned against his desk. "It sucks."

"It does." She half laughed. "The kicker is they promoted a supervisor on my team to take my place. The guy is barely twenty-two, and the whole reason my game had so much trouble. If I was a conspiracy theorist, I'd say he did it on purpose, but I have no proof. I only know something went down while I was away at the bachelorette weekend."

The one he'd convinced her to attend. She didn't say that, but he could tell she meant it.

"It's hard to believe being gone for two days

would change things so much."

"I'll never know now. Security stood by me while I cleaned my desk. They didn't let me say goodbye to anyone." Tears filled her eyes. She blinked. "I turned in my badge to HR and was escorted to my car."

He hugged her. "Do you want me to call Fritz?"

Dash wouldn't call the guy who founded her former company a close friend, but he was more than an acquaintance.

"I don't know if it would make a difference. I didn't see Fritz today, though I was told this came from the highest level which would be him, but thanks for offering." She sniffled. "But I could use your help."

Because this is your fault.

Dash didn't need to be a mind reader to sense that. "With what?"

She sat straighter. "Starting a gaming company."

He did a double take because she'd loved where she worked so much. "That's a big step."

Raina raised her chin. "I'm up for it, but I need funding."

His hinky meter kicked on. "Are you here for sympathy or money?"

She blinked her eyelashes before shrugging. "Both?"

Dash's cell phone buzzed. He rolled his eyes. No doubt his mom forgot to tell him something. He could deal with her later.

"Today's been rough on you," he said. "Take a few days to process things and clear your mind. Then, if you're serious about your own gaming company, put together a business plan, and I'll review it."

"I knew you'd help me."

"I didn't say yes."

"You will." She smiled. The tears had gone away. "You love gaming as much as I do. With your help, we can make this happen together."

With his money was what she meant. "It's getting late. I need to get out of here."

"Want to have dinner?" she asked, sounding hopeful.

He shook his head. "It's been a long day."

"Another time." She stood. "I'll be in touch."

As Raina left his office, he checked his phone. His mom hadn't texted him. It was Iris.

Iris: *Hey, I know work has slammed you this week, but it's 6:40, and you said you were picking me up at 6:30. Is everything okay?*

Oh, no. He was supposed to take Iris out to dinner tonight. He'd never confirmed their reservation. Probably a good thing he hadn't. He was in no shape to do anything but sleep.

Dash: *Sorry, I've been out of touch. Rough week at work. Little sleep. Parent hassles. Raina just left.*

Dash: *I won't be good company. Can we reschedule dinner tonight?*
Dash: *I promise I'll make it up to you.*

Dots appeared to tell him she was replying, but then they stopped.

Wait. There they were again.

Iris: *Get some sleep.*
Dash: *Thanks! You're the best.*

He waited for her reply. But no dots appeared.
No problem.
Dash yawned. He would talk to Iris tomorrow.

Chapter Sixteen

Holding her cell phone, Iris's hand trembled. Her breath hitched. As if in a daze, she forced herself to focus and reread Dash's text.

Dash: *Sorry, I've been out of touch. Rough week at work. Little sleep. Parent hassles. Raina just left.*
Dash: *I won't be good company. Can we reschedule dinner tonight?*
Dash: *I promise I'll make it up to you.*

Iris's stomach sank again. A lot was in his texts, but one thing wasn't.

Tears prickled. She blinked them away. Okay, tried. They kept welling in her eyes.

Having Dash cancel was bad enough, but he

hadn't wished her a happy birthday. Was he so tired he couldn't have typed two words? Or…

Iris plopped onto the consignment-shop-find couch delivered yesterday. She'd been feeling nothing but anticipation and excitement over today. How had she gone from expecting her best birthday ever to not having one?

This coming week is busy, but I'll make it up to you on Thursday. We'll do something extra-special.

Remembering Dash's words was like an icepick to her forehead. Not once had he mentioned her birthday when talking about Thursday. She'd made the leap to birthday. He…

Forgot.

Hurt slashed through her as if Dash had stuck a chef knife into her chest. She couldn't stop the tears. Not any longer. They fell from her face.

How could he forget the day in this age of digital calendars, social media, and reminders?

Iris didn't remember putting her birthday on his calendar before turning it over to Janice, but whether or not the date was on there didn't matter. Yes, he had many things on his mind, but he'd mentioned her birthday a few times last month.

Had he really forgotten?

He owed her nothing, but they'd been friends for over a decade and a half. He might not go all out each year, but he did something—a card with cash—because she had no one else in her life to remember her birthday.

Only Dash.

Starting at the top of her head and running to her toenails, fatigue overcame her. Heavy and exhausting. She closed her eyes, as if that could stop the truth.

He hadn't remembered.

He forgot.

The way he'd forgotten her at Christmas and the three years before that. Except, she realized ironically, for her birthday.

Yes, he'd worked nonstop this week, but he'd been in contact with his parents and seen his ex-girlfriend. He'd taken time for them, but not for Iris.

She wrapped her arms around her stomach that seemed to fill with heavy stones. The pain from her aching heart swamped her.

No matter how many times Dash promised to "make it up" to Iris, he hadn't followed through. Words were easy for him to say, but they were meaningless without the actions that came next. He claimed she was the most important person in his life, but what he did, especially tonight, proved otherwise.

She wasn't a priority.

His company, his parents, and his other friends were.

Iris thought about that—almost laughed at how history had repeated itself. Instead, she choked on a sob.

"How did I let this happen?"

This reminded Iris of her parents' restaurant, which had been their priority. She'd longed for more of her mom and dad's time, yet she never questioned their love for her. Sure, they didn't do the same things that other people did, but they included her in their passion for cooking, sharing their obsession with food. That was why she put her life on hold to take care of her mom and work at the restaurant to help her dad. Even knowing what her dad would end up doing, Iris wouldn't change her decisions because she'd loved them, and sometimes love meant making the hard choices—sacrifice.

Her gaze traveled back to Dash's text. She reread each line.

That was when she realized…

He hadn't only forgotten her birthday. He'd also forgotten their dinner date. If he'd remembered, he would have contacted her earlier, not wait to hear from her when he didn't show up.

In her heart of hearts, she knew what happened tonight was no different than before. His promises were empty ones. And his apologies had no meaning behind them.

Hot tears flowed.

Iris hated being treated this way. Yet, she kept letting him do it.

Why?

She'd only wanted to see the good in him.

Because you love him.

Iris stiffened. She did. She'd loved him forever. Probably from the day she met him when she was thirteen. The love had changed over the years, but it had remained a constant.

Hunching over, she sobbed.

Love wasn't a good reason to put up with this treatment.

Did Dash care for her?

Yes, she believed he did. Inviting her to stay. Putting her name on the title. Wanting to see where their friendship could go. All those things told her she meant something to him.

But it wasn't enough.

When Iris had decided to attend culinary school and move out, she'd known she had to rely on herself. Then Dash reappeared like the man she believed he could be. He'd captivated her. Only he wasn't that guy. He admitted he was selfish, but she hadn't listened. She should have because she deserved better.

Iris wiped her eyes.

She wanted to be with someone who built her up, made her a priority, and didn't make her feel as if her best traits were being easy going and not making waves. Once again, as during the past three years, she'd allowed this to happen by letting the fantasy of how she imagined things to be override the reality.

Her cell phone beckoned like a lighthouse in a dense fog.

Calling him now would be a mistake. She was too

emotional, and he was too tired. Tomorrow, she would talk to Dash.

In person.

Because she wanted…

Him.

No! She wanted closure.

She'd learned her lesson finally. Maybe Dash would learn one, too.

Doubtful.

He was Mr. Status Quo after all.

She sniffled.

No more tears.

Crying on one's birthday shouldn't be allowed. There should also be a rule about not being a hot mess, either. Iris had to do something to feel better.

Cake.

Chocolate cake always made things better.

Iris went into the kitchen. She would bake herself a birthday cake, and when she blew out the candle, she would make the best wish she could think of—to be with the man she loved and who loved her on her next birthday.

Twelve months from today.

Doable?

She had no idea because she would need time to get over Dash before she could love again.

Her heart wanted him, but he wasn't good for her.

Somehow, she had to move on from their

friendship and from him.

For good this time.

The idea was daunting, but she would survive the way she'd survived everything else.

Iris wouldn't give up. She had to believe something better was waiting for her, a person who would love her as fiercely as she loved them. They would be each other's priority, and she would have her happily ever. Remembering that would keep her going when the road got bumpy.

Like now.

Perhaps Hadley could offer advice. Iris might be on her own, but that didn't mean she couldn't reach out for help. And she would…at some point.

When she was ready.

She turned on the oven to preheat before removing her two round cake pans.

"Happy Birthday, Iris."

This wasn't the day she'd expected, but maybe it was what she needed to show her that she was worthy of so much more.

Of…love.

* * *

Friday morning, Dash arrived to work late. He hadn't set his alarm last night and told Janice not to wake him. He didn't want to start his and Iris's weekend in Hood Hamlet tired. He approached Fallon's desk.

"Anything I need to know?"

She glanced at a notepad. "Nothing pressing. Your three o'clock meeting is now at two-thirty. Oh, and your mom and your dad both called me wondering why you weren't returning their phone calls. I told them you were taking the morning off. I don't think they believed me."

He needed to tell his parents not to bug his assistant. "They don't always believe me, either."

"Good to know." Fallon studied him. "You look more rested."

"I feel human again. Sleep does wonders."

A brow arched. "You should make it a habit."

He laughed. "You think?"

"I'm serious, Dash. And while you're at it, coming in late every Friday."

"I *could* do that." But would he?

Wes had cut back his hours when he returned to work after his remission and recently resigned as CEO. The company's stock was doing well. Dash should ask how Wes was handling the changes.

"You should." Fallon's phone rang. "Let me know if you need anything."

A few minutes later, he sat at his desk, staring at his text messages. No morning selfie from Iris had arrived. That was weird. He typed.

Dash: *I'm no longer a sleep-deprived zombie. I should be home before six. When do you want to leave for Hood Hamlet?*

Iris: *I'll be at your house around six.*
Dash: *That works. Can't wait to see you. Have a wonderful day.*

He fired up his computer and got to work. That would make the time go faster.

A little before six, he pulled into the driveway. Iris's Range Rover sat on the left side, not in the garage, where it normally was. No problem. They could pull it inside before they left.

He parked next to her car. Leo had texted that he turned in the title to the DMV, and the new one would arrive in three to five weeks.

Inside, Dash found Iris sitting on a chair in the great room. She wore leggings and an oversized shirt. Not exactly snow weather attire, but she would be comfortable on the drive. She could change after they arrived.

He went to her, eager to make sure he didn't break their rule of greeting each other with a kiss. "Hey."

She crossed her arms over her chest. "We need to talk."

Not what he expected to hear. Her jaw was tight, and she wasn't smiling.

He stopped. Guess she wasn't as okay about last night as he thought she would be. "I'm sorry about canceling. I said we'd do something and then I was too tired. I will make it up to you. I promise."

"Stop." Her voice was harsher than he'd ever heard it. "Just stop, okay?"

"I said I was sorry." He hoped his voice conveyed his level of confusion.

"For the dinner."

Dash wanted to kiss away the hurt he saw in her eyes. "What else was there?"

"My birthday." Her lower lip quivered. "Yesterday was my birthday."

Air rushed from his lungs. He'd forgotten.

Dash stumbled back until his legs hit the couch, and he plopped onto the seat cushion. "I promised I'd make up for Christmas on your birthday, and I forgot."

It didn't matter that he'd been overworked, exhausted, or that Janice had taken "clear his calendar" literally. There wasn't an excuse for what he'd done. He'd failed Iris, hurt her, and she had every right to be upset.

"I shouldn't have forgotten, but I'll—"

Iris held up her hand. "No more false promises. It's too late."

His stomach clenched. A lump burned in his throat. "Too late for what?"

"Us."

A single word. Two letters. But the pain in her voice hit with the force of an 8.2 magnitude earthquake. If he hadn't been sitting, he would have fallen over.

He rubbed his hand over his face. "I made a mistake. It shouldn't have happened."

"But it keeps happening. The way it has before. And each time hurts more." The anguish in her voice made it hard for him to breathe. "I deserve better."

"You deserve the best. I want to give that to you. Be the best I can be. I…I care about you."

"I know you do."

That was a relief. He stood and paced across the great room. "Then what's the problem?"

"You don't care for me in the way I need. I need to be the priority. That's not something you can give me. I've known that since I was a teenager, but I forgot. I'm putting myself first." She wrung her hands. "I'm not willing to come after everything else in your life. I felt that way growing up, and I'm stopping the pattern before it gets any worse."

"You're not last."

"Your actions say differently. We'd made special plans. You hyped it up. And then you didn't even tell me it was off. I had to call you. Yet you had time for your parents and for Raina."

"I sent texts to my mom and dad." The words catapulted out. Dash had to show Iris she was wrong. Except all he'd done was proven she was right because he could have taken thirty seconds and contacted her. "I should have sent one to you."

She wrung her hands. "What happened with Raina?"

"She showed up at my office to tell me she'd been fired. I thought she needed a friend, but she wanted money to fund a gaming company. Your text arrived when I was talking to her. I thought it was my mom again, so I didn't check my phone until Raina left." Dash might not be helping his cause, but he would tell Iris the truth. That was the only way he could save what they had together. "I was so tired I didn't want to deal with anyone, including you. I just wanted to go home and sleep for the next twelve hours."

Iris stared at the rug in front of the fireplace with a faraway look in her eyes. "If I hadn't texted you, would you have contacted me?"

He hated hearing her hoarse voice. Not telling the truth would help his cause, but he couldn't. Being selfish hadn't served him. Neither had sticking with the status quo. She deserved honesty.

"No." Dash hadn't thought about Iris and their date. "I don't know how that happened. I was so excited after seeing you on Monday morning." He hung his head. "Exhaustion is no excuse, but I am sorry and I hope you forgive me."

"Thanks for being honest. Now it's my turn." She took a breath. "I've been falling for you. Hard. And it wasn't the first time. I knew about you being Mr. Status Quo, but I believed I was different from the other women you've dated."

"You are," he blurted. "You're my best friend."

Her gaze softened. "I was once upon a time. But

you're not that same boy, and I'm not that same girl. I thought we could have something special, but you made me feel less about myself. It wasn't just once. This was a pattern. I didn't have to be your top priority, but I needed to be on the list."

"You—"

"I wasn't," she interrupted. "You say all the right words, but you do nothing to back them up. Still, I accept your apology, and I hope you'll learn from this."

He clung to the glimmer of hope her words provided. "Does that mean you're giving me another chance?"

Regret shone in her eyes. "It means I'm breaking our deal. Both of them."

The air rushed from his lungs. His knees almost buckled. "No. We said friends forever."

"I agreed to that, but I…can't. I can't, because I can't see you as only a friend." Her chin trembled. "Last night, as I baked my own birthday cake and ate it by myself, I felt so alone in the world. I want more, Dash. I need more. A boyfriend. A ring on my finger. Marriage. Forever. These things don't appeal to you, but others might. I sure hope so, because I want you to have more, too."

This was killing him. She had it all wrong. "I want you."

"I'm sorry, but I can't keep doing this again when the outcome is the same. It's time, Dash. Time for each of us to find that special person who is out there for us." She lowered her gaze. "The keys to the Range Rover are on the island."

He couldn't lose his last tie to her. "I want you to have the car."

"I need to make a clean break." She sounded tired or maybe it was resigned. "This is for the best."

"Not for me. And not for you." He couldn't give up without a fight. "I hurt you. I disappointed you. You'll never know how much I regret doing that. Please don't end things like this. We belong together."

"I thought so, too, but not now. Thanks for everything. Take care of yourself. I… I hope you learn from this, too." She stood.

"Iris, please." His voice cracked.

"I know this hurts, but we'll get over it. Not today or next month or even six months from now, but eventually, it'll be okay."

Dash could barely breathe. His eyes burned. "This will never be okay."

Chapter Seventeen

Sunday afternoon, Dash found himself surrounded at his dining room table by his seven friends, who came bearing chicken wings, carrot and celery sticks, blue cheese and ranch dressings, sweet potato fries, and beer. He wasn't hungry—food and sleep didn't appeal to him lately—but he appreciated the thought. The others had no problem eating, and if they needed a new name for their group, he would suggest the Silicon Forest Piranhas. Now, if only he could convince them to leave.

"Delicious. And there are leftovers for when Wonderkid eats again." Henry wiped his mouth with a napkin. "The rest of us have finished our lunches, let's hear what happened with Iris."

Dash sipped from his beer. He couldn't look his

friends in the eyes. Not when he was embarrassed, heartbroken, and wracked with guilt.

Henry cleared his throat. "Dashiell."

Might as well just tell them. Dash sucked in a breath to give him strength. "On Friday, Iris broke up with me."

"What did you do?" Mason asked.

Dash frowned. "Why do you think I'm the one who did something?"

"Because it's Iris," Mason said. "And you're crazy about her."

Yeah. Dash was. "I canceled our dinner on Thursday."

"You've been working nonstop." Wes came to his defense. "You had to be exhausted."

"It was also her birthday, and I forgot."

The guys groaned.

"I'd promised to do something special for her birthday. To make up for forgetting about her at Christmas."

Kieran whistled. "Double whammy."

"I apologized, but she said it was too late." Saying that left a bitter taste in Dash's mouth.

"What else did she say to you?" Adam asked, his face sullen.

"Iris reminded me this has happened before. She's tired of my empty promises because my actions tell her she's not a priority in my life and she deserves better. She doesn't want to be friends. She claims she can't do that. She told me we'd both get over it, and we each had a special person out there for us. Oh, and she hopes I learn something from this."

Brett's gaze pinned Dash. "Have you?"

Dash nodded. "This has reaffirmed relationships aren't for me. I knew that after watching my parents' marriage disintegrate and the battles since then."

"You're not doomed to repeat what happened to your mom and dad." Blaise leaned back in his chair. "If that was the case, I'd be a junkie and likely dead."

"I don't know what a healthy relationship looks like," Dash explained. "My parents are still fighting, and both go through SOs at an alarming rate."

"Not everyone has good role models," Blaise admitted. "But you learn. I have, through trial and error. Thank goodness Hadley puts up with me."

"Hear, hear," all but Henry agreed.

"Many of us could say the same," Kieran added. "But what you can't do in a relationship is give up."

Dash rubbed his face. "She wants nothing to do with me. Becoming an obsessed stalker wouldn't endear me to the board or shareholders. Or her."

Mason nodded. "Truth."

"I've driven myself crazy thinking how this could have played out differently, but I was selfish. I forgot her birthday and our date. I broke my promise. And she's correct, it wasn't the first time, and she deserves better. You guys helped me in January, but this time, she's done. Nothing I do or say will change her mind."

"So you're giving up," Brett said in a matter-of-fact voice.

"What part of she doesn't want me in her life don't you get?" Dash asked.

Henry touched Dash's arm. "We're just trying to help."

Shame burned on his face. "I'm sorry. I've slept little this week."

"Or eaten," Adam said.

Dash nodded. "I blame myself. Iris told me what she expected. But I knew no matter what I did, she would be there. At least I thought she would be."

"Did you tell her you loved her?" Brett asked.

His mouth dropped open. "I… I didn't. I wasn't sure what I felt, but it was different with her than anyone else."

"Love," six of the seven spoke in unison. Only Henry remained silent.

Dash stared at each of his friends. "Would telling her have made a difference?"

"No one can know for certain," Kieran said.

"I should have told her, but after what I saw with my parents, I didn't believe love was possible." Dash rubbed his gritty eyes. "Now it's too late."

Henry tsked. "If you're giving up that easily, you don't deserve her."

Dash glared. "Haven't you done enough?"

"What's that supposed to mean?" Henry's

perplexed expression matched his voice.

"You kissed her on New Year's Eve. You convinced her to chase her dreams. You found her dad. You bought a building, so she'd have a place to live. Is there anything I missed?"

"Other than making sure Iris had a happy holiday while you were off celebrating Christmas with Raina, I'd say your list is complete."

Dash rolled his eyes. "If you hadn't—"

"She'd be sitting in that cottage in your backyard, trying to figure out what else you needed." Henry raised his voice. "Instead of pursuing her dreams and doing what would make her happy, she would be taking care of you. That you still want that tells me she's better off without you."

Each word hit, puncturing his heart like a bullet. Dash buried his head in his hands. "It's true. She is better off without me. But I'm not better off without her. I love her. But if this is how love feels, I want it to stop. I hate it."

Someone snickered—sounded like Mason. "It's not always like this."

"And it's never too late," Adam said. "Blaise…"

Dash glanced up.

Blaise raised his hand. "Trust me. It's never too late, or I wouldn't be with Hadley."

"Or me with Paige." Wes held up his hand.

Brett raised his. "I still don't know how Laurel forgave me, but I'm grateful each and every day."

Dash grimaced. "I'm not sure I'd forgive me if I was her."

"Come on," Mason encouraged. "Love conquers all."

"Even when stupid guys act like jerks," Blaise mumbled.

Dash stared at his beer. "I have no idea how to start."

"Make her dreams come true," Henry said.

Everyone looked at him, including Dash. "She's attending culinary school."

"That's only one dream." A mischievous smile spread across Henry's face. "Do you truly want Iris back in your life?"

"Yes," Dash croaked. "I'm barely functioning without her."

Henry eyed him warily. "What are you willing to do?"

"Anything it would take." Dash didn't hesitate answering.

Henry's mouth slanted. "Will you be patient?"

Dash cringed. That wasn't one of his strong points, but for Iris… "If I have to be, yes."

"Can you embrace change?"

That made him flinch. "I could, if I had to. Do you have an idea on how I can get Iris back in my life?"

"I do." A devilish gleam glinted in Henry's gaze. "But it will require a level of patience you've never imagined and a willingness to change. Not one thing, but multiple."

"I'll do it. Whatever it is, I'm in." The words poured from his lips like water from a firehose. "When she left, my life changed. I'm living in black and white. I want the color—I want her—back."

* * *

For Iris, Valentine's Day had always been a holiday other people celebrated. Most years, she'd ignored it unless she was dating someone. Which hadn't been often. But this February, every single pink or red heart captured her attention like a tractor beam. The cards, the candy, the flowers were everywhere, mocking her.

Seven days after breaking up with Dash, Iris's heart was still tender. She focused on her classes, which were going well, and she survived the fourteenth with only a few tears and several cupcakes.

A week later, Hadley reached out via text. Iris had no idea why the matchmaker wanted to meet, but she begged off. She wasn't ready to date, and given Hadley's sister was Dash's assistant, the temptation to ask about Dash would be strong.

Too strong.

Which was why Iris also asked Henry, who texted her almost daily, for more time before they met up in person again. She appreciated him checking in, but she needed to put Dash behind her.

Easier said than done.

By early March, Iris felt more like herself. Oh, her heart still missed Dash, but songs didn't trigger as many tears. When Hadley texted about having lunch again, Iris agreed.

That was how she found herself seated at a cute café in the heart of downtown on a Saturday. Instrumental music played. The servers wore white. She and Hadley each ordered a different quiche with a salad. The crust was flakey and the egg mixture tasty. The best part was Hadley not bringing up Dash. Hadley talked about her most recent trip to San Francisco, and Iris showed off the photos of her DIY projects for the apartment. They paid the check, splitting it at her insistence, so Iris was almost in the clear. She crossed her fingers.

Hadley lifted her glass of iced tea. "So, have you considered dating?"

Uh-oh. Maybe Iris had spoken too soon.

"I haven't." She took a sip of her strawberry lemonade. "I'm doing better than I was in February. My focus is school."

"You look beautiful."

Heat rushed up Iris's neck. That was a compliment coming from Hadley, who dressed nicely even on a Saturday. "Would you want to go on a date?"

"I…" Iris's instinct was to say no, but… "Maybe. I'm still getting over what happened, and I'm not sure if I should be completely over Dash before I date again."

"That is an individual's choice. Some enjoy jumping into the dating pool immediately. Others wait weeks, months, even years." Hadley took a sip. "If you want to dip your toe into the water, I have a client who might be a solid match for you."

This sounded familiar. "The same guy you mentioned before?"

"No, he would have been an excellent choice for you, but he's seriously dating another person I introduced him to." Hadley's smile lit up her face. "I have a feeling an engagement will be announced soon."

Whoa. Iris's "serious" dating was limited, but she couldn't imagine getting engaged so quickly. "Congrats, but that was fast."

"Sometimes people click. That's the case here. And I must admit, I get chills when it happens." Hadley stared over the lip of her glass. "Think you want to meet him?"

"I don't know if my heart will be in it." Dash was still on her mind a lot. Though not as much as before. "I don't want to lead anyone on."

"The first meetings are low-key, usually coffee. It's a safe and comfortable date with a limited time commitment so you can check each other out. In your case, it would be a good way to put yourself out there again and get back into the feel of dating."

She couldn't believe she was considering this, but maybe this would help her to move forward. "So no expectations from either party?"

"None," Hadley said. "And you'd be doing me a favor."

Iris twirled her straw. "How so?"

"This client has specific requirements."

That sounded weird. "Such as?"

"A foodie."

"At least we'd have something to talk about."

"Right?" Hadley laughed. "Another is, loves chocolate."

"Who doesn't love chocolate?" Henry had sent her a box of chocolates from Welton Wines and Chocolate in Hood Hamlet. They'd been scrumptious. "But I guess that's another thing we have in common that we could discuss."

"Believes in happily ever afters."

"Wow." She couldn't believe a guy would have that as a requirement. "I must admit I'm intrigued now."

Hadley leaned forward over the table. "So is that a yes?"

"I…" Iris hesitated, weighing the pros and the cons. The biggest knowing she would be dating someone who wasn't Dash. "Just coffee?"

Hadley nodded.

One date couldn't hurt. "Okay, yes."

***

Three days later, Iris hurried to a locally owned coffee shop two blocks from her apartment. She wanted to arrive early, so she could order a drink and find a seat before she met EC, Hadley's client, who was described as being tall and handsome.

An excellent combination, but Iris wished she knew something more specific about the guy. Hadley said he would recognize her and not to worry.

Easier said than done.

Inside the coffee shop, jazz music played. Smiling people occupied a few tables. Iris hoped she would smile soon, but she bit her lip instead. When she reached the counter, she ordered a chai latte. If the meeting got awkward, or she bolted, she didn't want EC to have paid for her.

A few minutes later, Iris grabbed her drink and sat at a table. The interior was small enough that anyone who walked in could see her.

A text notification buzzed.

She glanced at her phone.

Hadley: *Relax and have fun. It's just coffee.*
Iris: *I'm trying.*
Hadley: *I'll check in later.*
Iris: *Thanks.*

Seeing an email notification, she clicked her

THE DEAL BREAKER

inbox.

"Iris Jacobs?" a familiar male voice asked.

A shiver ran along her spine.

No, it couldn't be him.

Slowly, as if she could avoid the inevitable, she glanced up from her phone. Not surprisingly, a smiling Dash stood next to her table.

Still, her mouth gaped. She felt dizzy.

Where had he come from? What was he doing here?

And why did he look hotter?

Okay, he'd always been gorgeous, but this appeared to be Dash 2.0. He looked…healthier, as if he'd been working out and spending time outside.

This so wasn't fair.

Wait. That couldn't be Dash. She had to be hallucinating.

Iris blinked. Once. Twice.

Nope. He was still there.

"Dash?" Flutters erupted in her stomach. She glanced around, but didn't see any other men entering the shop. Good, her date must be running late. "What are you doing here?"

"Hi." He extended his hand, but she was too stunned to shake it. "I'm EC."

"You're Hadley's client?" she screeched.

He nodded.

Iris didn't know if she should laugh or cry. Or why Hadley would have done this. It had to go against the matchmaker's code. Well, if one existed. "Why did you do this?"

"Ask me what EC stands for?"

Iris swallowed around the lump in her throat. "What does the EC stand for?"

"Embracing Change, but you can call me Dash."

She stared, dumbfounded.

"You already have a drink," he said, acting as if what was happening was normal. "I'm going to order something. Please stay."

She doubted she could move from being in shock. Iris nodded once.

Dash got in line.

Her cellphone buzzed.

Henry: *Trust me, it'll be okay. Give Dash a chance.*
Iris: *How do you know what's going on?*
Henry: *I'm here, in case you need me.*

Iris scanned the other tables until she saw a man dressed like the ultimate Blazers fan. She'd never seen Henry dressed so casually or wearing a baseball cap, but even his tennis shoes were team colors. He looked like he should be at the Moda Center cheering on Portland's basketball team to victory.

He blew her a kiss.

Her phone buzzed again.

Henry: *Breathe, Iris.*

THE DEAL BREAKER

Iris: *I don't know if I can do this.*
Henry: *You can and you will.*
Henry: *But if you need me, just say, "Oh, Henry."*

Dash returned with a coffee and sat. "You probably want an explanation."

Under the table, she wiggled her fingers to keep from freaking out. "That would be helpful."

"The simple answer is I wanted to see you." His mouth quirked. "The complicated one is I know I screwed up and don't deserve the chance to talk to you again, but I had to try."

She let his words soak in. "So you enlisted Hadley…"

"That part was Henry's idea. Most of this was, but he was right," Dash admitted. "Hadley first said no. She wanted no part of this, but after she compared our two questionnaires and realized we were a match, she agreed."

"I feel set up."

"You were, but I didn't think you'd see me otherwise."

Iris couldn't believe he'd done this. "I wouldn't have."

"I accept that. Even after you gave me another chance, I didn't learn my lesson. Everything was still all about what I wanted. Not what was best for you or us."

"Then why are you here now?"

"To tell you I'm embracing change after losing you," he admitted. "Not that I'm changing for you. I'm doing it for me. To be a better person. Lesson learned the hard way."

Mission accomplished, but it was bittersweet. "You look different. Healthier."

And hotter.

Iris didn't dare say it. She wasn't sure thinking it was smart, either.

His eyes brightened. "I hired a personal trainer. I've given Tony full reign to make nutritious meals, and I'm learning to tolerate vegetables. I'm working set hours, going in late on Fridays, and sleeping more."

"It shows."

"Thanks. And I mean that. If not for you, I would have never done this."

"I'm happy for you." Except… "I should have—"

"You tried. Remember the zucchini bread? Asking me to go hiking? Slow down? I was too set in my ways, thinking that was the only way because I was being stupid." He sipped his coffee. "I also dealt with my parents."

She fought the urge to shred the napkin under her cup. That might stop her from fidgeting so much. "What do you mean?"

"Being constantly put in the middle of them wore me out. Their nitpicking and fighting kept getting worse. It was wearing on me, and I realized it couldn't continue. I sold the beach house, bought them each one of their own, and set up two trusts, complete with pool boy and bimbo clauses in case they remarry. All requests for money go through the trustee, not me. If one mentions the other to me, in any form of communication, ten thousand dollars from his or her account will be deposited into the other's. So far it's working well."

"Wow." That was a bigger surprise than all the other changes, but they all equaled one thing. "Goodbye, Mr. Status Quo."

"Hello, EC." He laughed, though it sounded forced.

"This might sound weird, but I'm proud of you."

Dash sucked in a breath. "Not weird. That means so much to me. Thank you."

His sincerity was apparent in his voice and gaze.

Too much. Seeing him so happy was wonderful, and the only thing she'd wanted for him, but it was too much. Emotionally, she couldn't take any more.

Her eyelids grew hot.

Oh, no. She needed to get out of here. "Thanks for going to so much trouble to see me. I'm happy to see the changes. But I have to leave."

As she went to scoot back, he held her hand. "Wait."

The corners of her eyes prickled. She blinked before looking up at the ceiling, trying to keep the tears at bay.

He let go of her hand. "Please."

Dash might have changed, but years of doing what she could to make him happy had her staying.

She clasped her hands on her lap. "Why?"

He blew out a breath. "Showing you I was working to be a better person was only one part of wanting to see you tonight."

Her pulse skittered. "What was the other?"

"I want us to start over. That's why I introduced myself when I showed up."

She stared into her drink. "As friends."

"As more."

Iris jerked up her gaze to meet his. "More?"

"I'm ready. Truly ready. I won't make any promises because I might still screw up. But I will do my best to not repeat the same mistakes. And will put you first. The way you have since we met."

Tears welled, and she rubbed her eyes. "I want to believe you."

"Don't."

She flinched. "What?"

"You've believed in me and trusted me, and I've let you down so many times. You don't need to do that again." He took a breath. "Instead, let me show you what I mean and feel for you. One step, one day, at a time."

Her heart pounded so hard she struggled to breathe. "Really?"

He nodded. "You're my special person, Iris. And

I'm yours, but you don't have to take my word for it. I'll prove it's true, if you let me."

A part of her was afraid of being hurt again, but if she didn't take that chance, she might regret it for the rest of her life.

"OK, EC." She lifted her chin. "Prove it."

Chapter Eighteen

Dash paced across the length of the restaurant's dining area, wringing his hands and fighting nerves.

"Stop pacing!" Mason yelled as he helped Rachael add the finishing touches to the romantic table for two in the restaurant. "Everything will go perfectly because my beautiful wife is the best event planner in the Pacific Northwest."

"Awww." Rachael kissed her husband on the cheek. "Now put the knives in the correct position."

Dash stopped. "Dude. Don't mess this up for me."

Mason grinned. "Iris will be so overwhelmed she won't notice the knives, dude."

"You need to fix them." Rachael shot a you're-going-to-mess-this-up-so-do-it look to her husband.

"On it," Mason said.

Dash paced again. He flexed his fingers to see if that helped him relax.

"Relax." Kieran carried a bottle of champagne to the kitchen where Tony and Janice were cooking the special seven-course dinner. "Things are going well between the two of you, right?"

"Yes." After the night at the coffee shop at the beginning of March, they'd grown closer. Their relationship was better than he imagined, and that was saying a lot. It was now May, and though some might say it was a little quick, they'd known each other for fifteen years. Dash had been patient. But he was tired of waiting. He wanted to make more of Iris's dreams come true. Especially since they were now his dreams, too.

Blaise laughed. "When I suggested a grand gesture, I had no idea you'd come up with this."

Oh, no. Dash glanced around the restaurant. "Is it not enough?"

His friends laughed.

Leo adjusted Dash's tie. "It's perfect."

Paige squeezed his arms. "You'll blow Iris away."

"You did good, Wonderkid," Wes agreed.

Adam surveyed the dining area. "I don't care what you guys said. We could have easily rigged up a fireworks show in here."

"No!" everyone shouted.

Cambria sighed. "The only fireworks needed will be from kisses."

Selah nodded. "And that won't be a problem with these two."

Laurel pushed Noelle's stroller back and forth. "Real sparks would interfere with the cameras."

Dash startled. "Cameras as in plural?"

"Trust the sole dad in the group." Brett clapped Dash's shoulder. "I've got them positioned so you'll have multiple angles."

Dash gulped. "Okay."

At least he hoped it would be.

"T-minus two minutes," Laurel announced. "Everyone except Dash in the kitchen."

His friends filed past, giving him high fives or fist bumps.

"Good luck."

"Don't sweat it."

"You've got this."

"You're putting us all to shame, Wonderkid."

"Smile."

"Breathe."

Suddenly, it was only him standing there with a single table in the center of the dining area. Dash had no doubts about his relationship with Iris. He could visualize their future together. His nerves stemmed from wanting to make tonight perfect for her.

Calling this a real life fairy tale might be too much, but for the past two months he'd been showing her what she meant to him, and he wanted her to know he would do that until he took his last breath.

"It's almost time," Hadley called from the kitchen.

He inhaled deeply and then exhaled. On that dreary Sunday in February, when he told his friends about Iris breaking up with him, Mason had said that love conquers all.

Dash hadn't believed him. His parents fighting and their divorce had tainted love. But thanks to Iris and her forgiving heart, he now believed.

His friends had helped him become a better person, a man who deserved the love of a woman like Iris. Today, they were all here, helping him to take the relationship to the next level.

All he needed was for Iris to arrive so they could get started.

* * *

Iris sat next to Henry in the back of his limousine. She had no idea where they were going or why she had to be here, but he'd been adamant she come with him. Not that she minded being out and about this Saturday. Dash was getting together with a couple of the guys, so she would have just been reading or cooking in her apartment.

Henry stretched out his legs. His leather shoes

appeared newly polished. "Did you hear Paige and Wes set a wedding date?"

"I hadn't." She'd been too busy at the culinary school and spending every free minute with Dash. She hadn't seen his friends since a dinner in April. He'd more than shown Iris how much she meant to him, and she knew she was a priority, if not his top one. "That's great. I'm sure it'll be a lovely wedding. When is it?"

"July eighteenth."

"July," she repeated. If all six married before Adam's first anniversary on July thirteenth, they would call off the bet and split the fund. Though for a billionaire, losing an extra hundred or hundred-and-fifty million might not be a big deal.

Forget first world problems. This was a one percent problem.

"I always knew Dash would win the bet," Henry said.

"Me, too." She'd known all along he'd be the last single man standing. "I doubt the money means as much to him as the bragging rights."

"I believe you are correct."

Iris glanced out the side window. "Hey, this is the neighborhood where I grew up."

"Really?" Henry sounded surprised. "I had no idea."

She nodded. "After the rejuvenation a few years ago, it's trendy now."

The limo stopped. Frank got out and then opened the passenger door.

Iris found herself on the sidewalk outside the restaurant her parents once owned and where they'd lived above it.

She struggled to breathe.

In-out. In-out.

She'd avoided this part of town for years because it hurt too much to remember. Every day, she missed her mom. She rarely thought about being pushed out of her dad's life so easily now. But occasionally, Iris even missed him. Despite the choices he'd made, she hoped he wasn't living with regrets.

Standing here brought back so many feelings. Each breath seemed to take a conscious effort and hurt. She expected tears to fill her eyes, but none came. Only a sense of loss did. One that still cut deep.

"What are we doing here?" Iris whispered, afraid if she spoke louder she might awaken more memories and the ghosts that accompanied them.

A serious expression crossed his face.

"Henry?" she asked.

"I hope this doesn't hurt too much." Compassion shone in his hazel-green eyes. "You're thinking about your parents."

Of course he would understand. She tried to nod but couldn't because the pain was too raw, too sharp, even if it was six years old. "I haven't been back here since the day my father kicked me out."

Henry hugged her. "Places trigger memories. Focus on the happy ones. And perhaps you can replace the not-so-good memories with better ones."

She doubted that. "Please tell me what we're doing here."

"You'll see." Henry opened the door for her.

Iris froze at the threshold. Her insides twisted. She never thought she'd step foot inside again, but she forced herself to move.

A romantic ballad played. "I didn't know you enjoyed this kind of music."

Henry shrugged. "I'm a connoisseur of all types."

The paint color had changed. The hostess stand was missing. Only one table was in the dining room, a stunningly set table for two with a linen tablecloth, flowers, candles, crystal stemware, and fine china place settings.

She glanced at Henry. "What's going on?"

"I don't think I've mentioned it, but you remind me a little of Cinderella, only with an evil father and no horrible stepsisters. You don't have a fairy-godmother, but you do have me, who's on a first-name basis with every salesperson at Tiffany's."

Iris laughed, feeling more at ease.

"Don't think too much, okay?" He kissed her cheek. "And enjoy yourself, princess."

With that, he and Frank went to the kitchen.

Someone cleared his throat.

She turned toward the sound and saw Dash. He

wore a dark gray suit with a white dress shirt, a yellow tie covered with video game controllers, and leather shoes. He greeted her with a kiss. Shorter than most, but equally hot.

The painful memories faded. Her heart swelled with love. "I should have known you were involved, but what is all this?"

His grin crinkled the corners of his eyes. "A little something I dreamed up for us."

"I like the sound of us."

He laced his fingers with hers and led her toward the table. "The first time you brought me into this restaurant, we were thirteen. You introduced me to your mom and dad as your new friend. But even back then, I wanted to be your boyfriend. I just didn't have a clue what I was feeling."

Iris squeezed his hand. "I'm happy you figured it out."

"Me, too. You're the best thing in my life." He brushed his lips over hers.

"Tease."

He laughed. "My parents and your dad weren't good role models, but we're not them. We don't have to follow in their footsteps. And we haven't, which is why we share an amazing love."

Joy brimmed inside her. "I love you."

"I love you." He swallowed, seeming nervous. "You helped me make my dreams come true. If you hadn't been there every step of the way, either long distance when I was in college or right next to me at home supporting me, I wouldn't be the founder of a successful company. Even when you were taking care of your mom and working the dinner shift here, you'd bring me a meal, so I wouldn't go hungry."

"You can't live off fruit snacks and soda."

"I know." He laughed. "You gave, gave, gave until I realized I needed to do the same."

She gazed up at him, hoping he could feel her love flowing from her to him. "You have. These past months…"

"It's only the beginning." He motioned to the dining area. "This was your home, where you grew up, and where we became friends."

"You made it not so lonely for me."

"And you gave me a sanctuary to escape my parents' arguing." He reached into his jacket pocket, removed a set of keys, and placed them in the palm of her hands. "The restaurant is yours now. The way it should have been six years ago when your father left town."

"You remembered my dream."

Dash nodded.

Her breath caught in her throat. Her eyes stung. "I don't know what to say."

He held her close, his warmth and strength soothing the emotions tumbling inside her. "Don't say anything. Your eyes and expression tell me what this means to you, and I'm so happy to do this for you."

"For us, right?"

"Yes, for us." Laughter lit his eyes. "And I hope you're not saying this because of all the remodeling it needs."

She grinned. "Now that you mention it…"

"There's no rush. We can go slow." He ran a finger along her jawline. "I figure we have until you graduate from culinary school."

"Sounds perfect." It really did. She glanced at the table. "Is that for our celebration dinner?"

"Yes, but I want to do one more thing first." He dropped onto his knee before removing something else from his jacket pocket—a ring box.

She gasped, clutching the keys in her right hand.

"I love you, Iris Jacobs. You have my heart. That will always belong to you. I can't imagine my future without you by my side." He opened the top to show a large diamond in a platinum setting. "Will you marry me?"

Butterflies erupted in her stomach. Tingles spread outward from her chest. "Yes. A billion times, yes."

A collective sigh sounded from the kitchen.

Dash slid the ring on her left hand finger. A perfect fit.

"It's stunning."

"Not compared to you." Dash kissed her and then drew back. "Now it's time for our celebration dinner."

She stared at the elegant diamond, the facets

shooting colorful prisms around the room. "And then what happens?"

"We kiss." He pressed his forehead against hers. "And then we live happily ever after."

"And have lots of children!" Henry yelled from the kitchen.

She and Dash laughed.

She gazed up at him. The love reflected in his eyes echoed her own. "I'm game."

He kissed her. "Same."

"Order up," someone in the kitchen called out. Tony, perhaps?

"I think that's our cue to sit," she said.

"Fine." Dash pulled out a chair for her. "But I need a raincheck on more kisses."

"You can have as many as you want for as long as you want."

Dash grinned. "I'm holding you to that."

Iris sighed. She kind of felt like Cinderella minus the glass slipper, but she got something so much better than Prince Charming—Dash.

And she wouldn't change a thing.

Epilogue

June 27th

Henry loved June weddings. Who was he kidding? Nuptials were his favorite event to attend, and this one…

He raised his champagne flute for a toast. Not to the bride and the groom who, with both of their hands on a silver cutter, sliced into the elaborate tiered wedding cake. No, this toast was for him.

I did it again.

Feeling as buoyant as the bubbles floating to the top of his glass, his smile widened.

Once again, his mad matchmaking skills had brought a couple together. The love radiating from Iris and Dash made up for Henry's frustration over the groom taking so long to see what was in front of him. His friend had needed a push—okay, a shove. A big one from Henry, and making his green-eyed monster take control had worked better than expected. Not his usual method to bring two people together, but a necessary one to show Dash the love of his life had been right under his nose since he was thirteen.

Henry had nothing against Raina, but she hadn't been the right woman for Wonderkid. Dash needed someone who saw past his net worth and brilliant brain to the man inside. Iris, sweet-wonderful-caring-cooks-like-a-dream Iris, was that person. She always would be today, tomorrow, and every day after that. Thank goodness Henry and the others could help them resolve their differences and reunite. Otherwise, none of them would be here celebrating.

A satisfied feeling flowed through Henry. His success rate with couples should worry Hadley Mortenson, but he wouldn't rub it in. Not at the reception. But perhaps at the brunch tomorrow.

Today, he would revel in his latest accomplishment.

Thanks to him, another billionaire of Silicon Forest would live happily ever after. Only one remained single—Wes—which meant he won the bet, but he and Paige would say "I do" on July eighteenth.

Well, done, Davenport.

He raised his glass slightly before sipping the

expensive bubbly. Delicious. Champagne tasted better at weddings.

As the crowd cheered, Iris and Dash stared lovingly at one another. Then, each took a piece of cake and served it to the other. Politely. No teasing or smashing the cake into the other's face. That boded well for the future according to an article Henry had read about lasting relationships. Like his other matches, this one would last.

Knowing that pleased him more than all the money in the world—and he had a good chunk of that in his bank and investment accounts. But Henry wanted to learn everything he could to make sure his friends remained happily married. That was the least he could do for the people who were now his family.

Well, the closest thing he had to one.

Hope you're finally proud of me, Mom and Dad.

Henry took another sip.

Now, to figure out how to follow this up…

Ideas flowed through his head.

Blaise strode up to him, wearing what appeared to be a new tuxedo. No doubt, Hadley's influence. "You're gloating."

"I believe the correct term is glowing," Henry said.

"No." Blaise studied him. "Definitely gloating."

Henry raised his glass. "What can I say? I'm a matchmaker extraordinaire."

Blaise raised a brow. "No, that's my wife."

"Hadley is known as the Wife Finder. She's paid for her services. Me? I do this out of the goodness of my heart. That's why I deserve a bigger title, especially since I'm the one who told you to call her."

"Touché." Blaise laughed. "So what will you do now that we've all found the love of our lives?"

With his free hand, Henry tapped the side of his head. "I already have a plan. You guys are only one friend group. I have others, and many who need my services. Unlimited possibilities for more weddings and godchildren."

Blaise shook his head. "Quit while you're ahead."

"Where's the fun in that?" Henry drank more champagne.

"What about you?" Blaise asked.

"*Moi?*"

"When are you going to fall in love and settle down?"

Henry shrugged and repeated what he'd been telling himself for years. "I'm happy being single. Besides, it wouldn't be fair to the women of the world for me to just pick one to be with."

Wes joined them. "When you meet the one, you'll want to put a ring on her finger so fast your head will spin."

"My head hasn't and won't ever spin, but I'm ecstatic that happened to you." Henry hated seeing his friend so sick, but he loved seeing him so happy and healthy now. He raised his champagne to Wes. "And you won the last single man standing bet. Congratulations."

Blaise and Wes exchanged an odd glance, telling Henry something was up.

Wes smiled. "Thanks, but I'm not claiming the fund."

That surprised Henry given the amount of money at stake. "Why not?"

"I spoke with Paige and then the others. We've decided to use the fund to create a new philanthropic endeavor. We're calling it the Silicon Forest Friends Foundation."

Henry's breath hitched. He blinked to stop the stinging in his eyes. "That's the most wonderful thing I've heard since Iris and Dash's 'I do.'"

Blaise touched Henry's shoulder. "I'll continue to manage the fund. Brett has joined the foundation's board of directors, and we would like you on it, as well."

A lump formed in Henry's throat. More happiness flowed through him. "Yes. Thank you. I'm honored."

"Oh," Wes said. "Clear your calendar for next weekend."

"Party at the Lockhart house?"

"No." Mischief filled Wes's eyes. "A wedding in Lake Tahoe."

"Wedding? I thought you had a big one planned for July."

"We do, but we only picked that date to accommodate Paige's brother. We don't want to wait so we're having something more intimate."

"You're eloping," Henry whispered.

Wes nodded. "I'd like you to be my best man, so you'd better be there."

Henry's tight chest made breathing difficult. This was turning into the second best day ever. The first was when his goddaughter, Noelle, had been born. Though Brett and Laurel's wedding was wonderful. As was Blaise and Hadley's. And all the others.

"I…" He cleared his throat. "Of course I'll be there. I'm happy to fly whoever needs a ride on my plane."

"Thank you." Wes beamed. "I can't say that enough because you're the reason I was at the Christmas party and saw Paige. Without you…"

Relishing in the compliment, Henry touched Wes's arm. "That's what friends are for."

"I'll send you details tomorrow." Wes waved to Paige. "Right now, I owe a special someone a dance."

Blaise nodded. "Hadley's motioning to me."

"Go. Don't keep your ladies waiting." Henry took another sip of his champagne. "I need to decide who gets the next dance with me."

A few single women were in attendance. Several from the restaurant industry, and others who worked with Dash. A few had known the couple in high school.

THE DEAL BREAKER

Henry downed what remained in his glass. Frank would pick him up tonight, so nothing limited his number of drinks. Well, other than finding the server walking around with the glasses and bottle.

"Having fun?" a familiar male voice asked.

Henry turned to see Dash and Iris, who held hands. Their faces glowed. "Yes, I was just deciding who to dance with next."

Dash raised their linked hands and kissed Iris's. "I already danced with my mom. The rest belong to my wife."

Iris laughed. "That's like the hundredth time you've said wife today."

Dash shrugged. "I like the sound of it."

She rose on her toes and kissed him. "So do I."

"I knew you would be perfect together," Henry admitted. "But sometimes, it's hard to see what's right in front of you. Which was why I took matters into my own hands."

"Wait." Dash's brow wrinkled. "You played matchmaker with us?"

Henry nodded. "I may have taken advantage of that green-eyed monster inside of you, Master Dashiell, on New Year's Eve."

Iris's mouth gaped. "Dash was the person you were trying to make jealous?"

"Yes." Satisfaction and pride puffed Henry's chest. "And it worked beautifully."

Dash shook his head. "I can't believe you did all that."

"Believe it."

As Iris gazed into her groom's eyes, love flowed between them.

Yes, Henry done well with this pair.

He shrugged. "What can I say? It worked."

Iris shimmied her shoulders. "It did. Saying thank you isn't enough."

"Then just remember who's earned the right to be the godfather of all babies you have." The thought of more godchildren made him giddy. "Sweet Noelle needs playmates, and I need more little ones to spoil."

"What happens if you meet someone and fall in love?" Iris asked.

Dash nodded. "You might not have as much time for godfathering."

Henry shook his head. "I'll always have time for that. Besides, I don't see myself as a boyfriend or husband."

Iris leaned into Dash. "That doesn't mean it won't happen."

Dash kissed Iris on the lips. "You asked me to trust you, Henry. Trust me when I say there's nothing like falling in love, especially with your best friend."

The two were adorable with their heart eyes for each other.

"One never knows what will happen." Henry said that for their benefit since it was Iris and Dash's wedding day. He snagged a full glass of champagne from a passing server and held it up. "To living happily ever after with your one true love."

Henry's godfather role could expand if these two and the others did their part, as he hoped they would. Uncle Henry had a catchy ring, and only his natural ability with children surpassed his matchmaking skills. Henry had no idea what the future held for any of them, including himself, but he couldn't wait to find out.

About The Author

USA Today bestselling author Melissa McClone has written over forty-five sweet contemporary romance novels. She lives in the Pacific Northwest with her husband, three children, two spoiled Norwegian Elkhounds, and cats who think they rule the house. They do!

If you'd like to find Melissa online:
www.melissamcclone.com
www.facebook.com/melissamcclonebooks
www.facebook.com/groups/McCloneTroopers
twitter.com/melissamcclone
www.instagram.com/melmcclone

Other Books By Melissa McClone

STANDALONE

A matchmaking aunt wants her nephew to find love under the mistletoe…
The Christmas Window

SERIES
All series stories are standalone, but past characters may reappear.

The Billionaires of Silicon Forest
The Wife Finder
The Wish Maker
The Deal Breaker

Quinn Valley Ranch
Relatives in a large family find love in Quinn Valley, Idaho…
Carter's Cowgirl
Summer Serenade

Beach Brides and Indigo Bay Sweet Romance Series
A mini-series within two multi-author series…
Jenny
Sweet Holiday Wishes
Sweet Beginnings

Her Royal Duty
Royal romances with charming princes and dreamy castles...
The Reluctant Princess
The Not-So-Perfect Princess
The Proper Princess

One Night to Forever Series
Can one night change your life…
and your relationship status?
Fiancé for the Night
The Wedding Lullaby
A Little Bit Engaged
Love on the Slopes
The One Night To Forever Box Set: Books 1-4

Mountain Rescue Series
*Finding love in Hood Hamlet with a
little help from Christmas magic…*
His Christmas Wish
Her Christmas Secret
Her Christmas Kiss
His Second Chance
His Christmas Family

Ever After Series
Happily ever after reality TV style…
The Honeymoon Prize
The Cinderella Princess
Christmas in the Castle

Love at the Chocolate Shop Series
Three siblings find love thanks
to Copper Mountain Chocolate…
A Thankful Heart
The Valentine Quest
The Chocolate Touch

The Bar V5 Ranch Series
Fall in love at a dude ranch in Montana…
Home for Christmas
Mistletoe Magic
Kiss Me, Cowboy
Mistletoe Wedding
A Christmas Homecoming